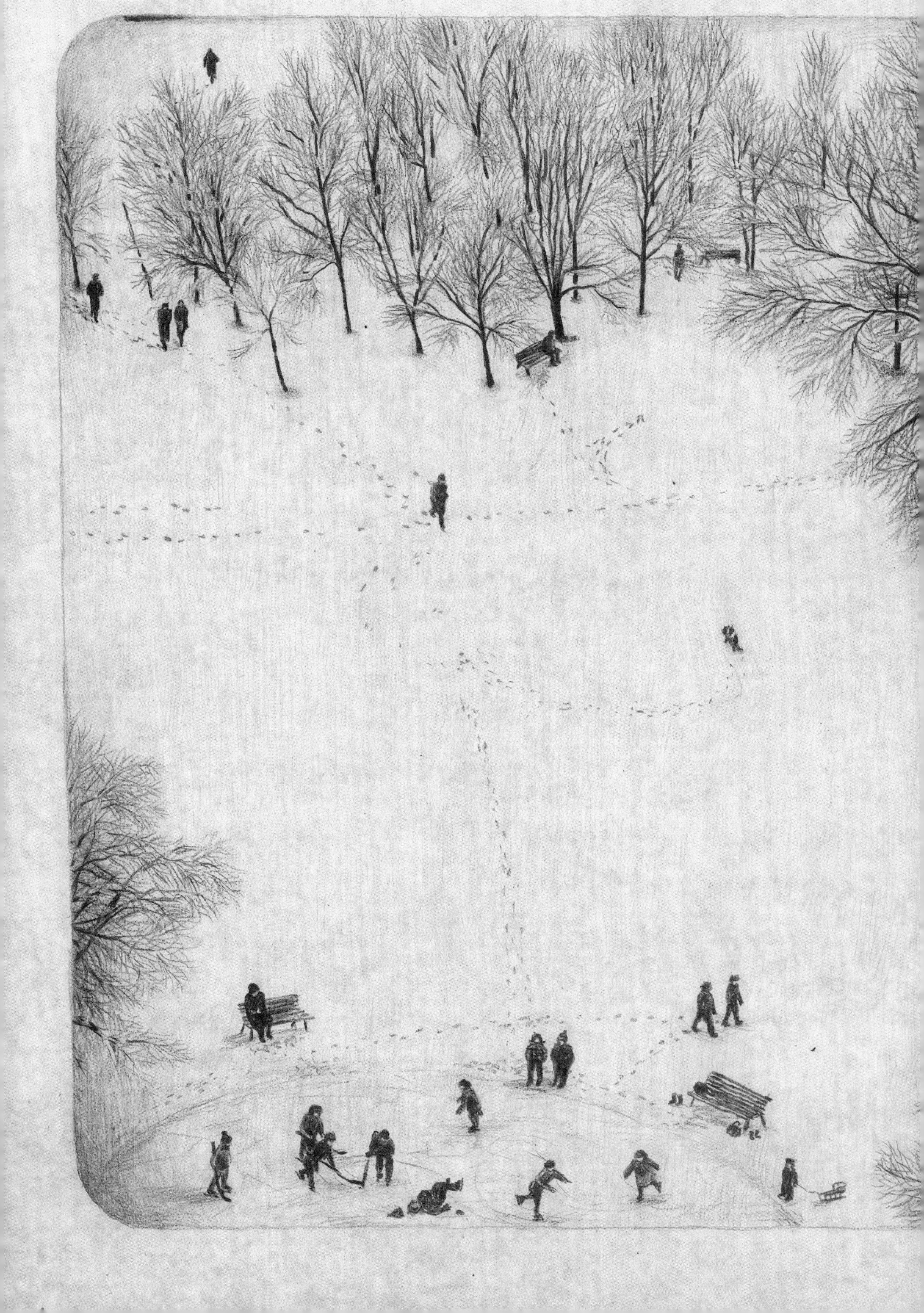

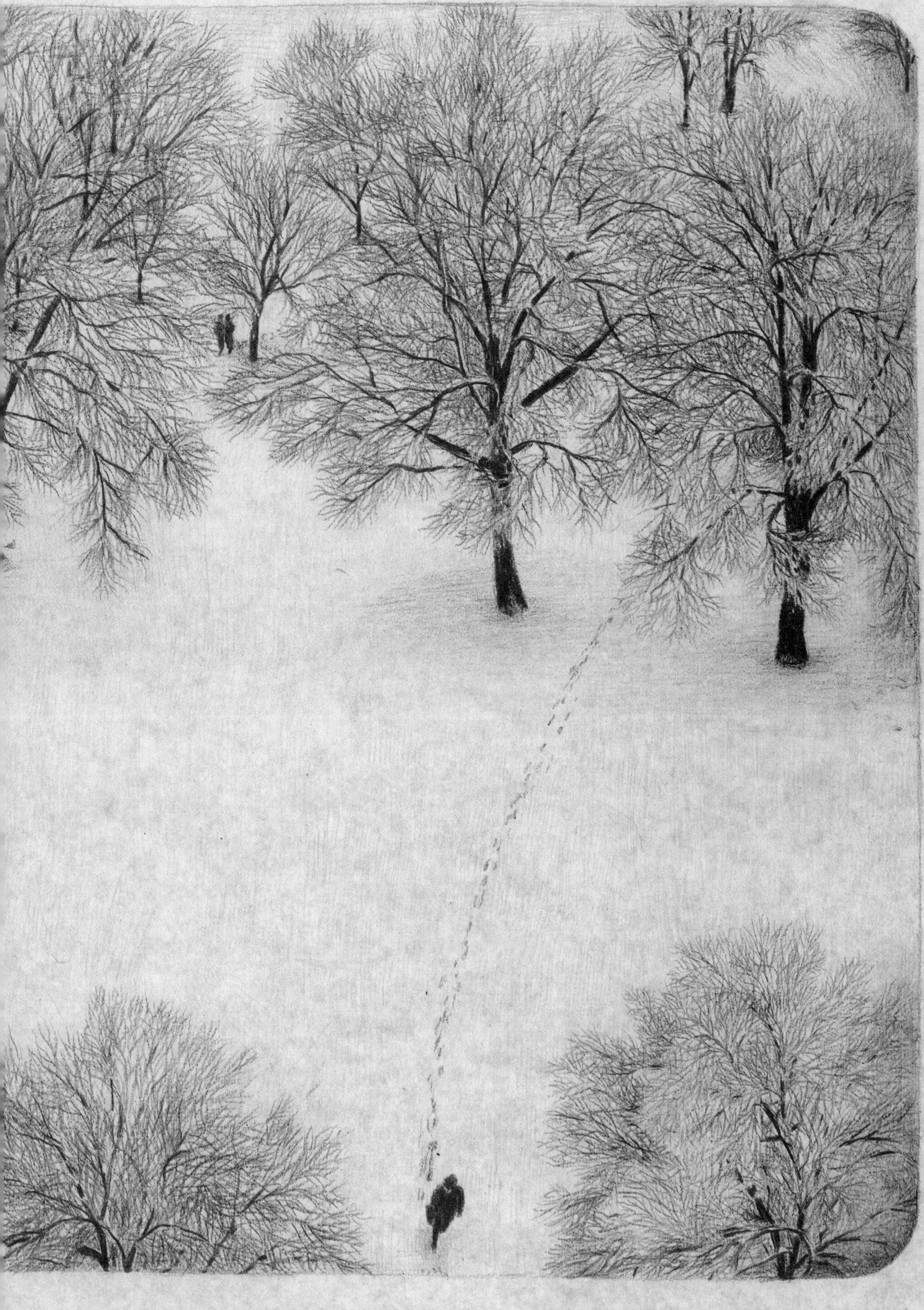

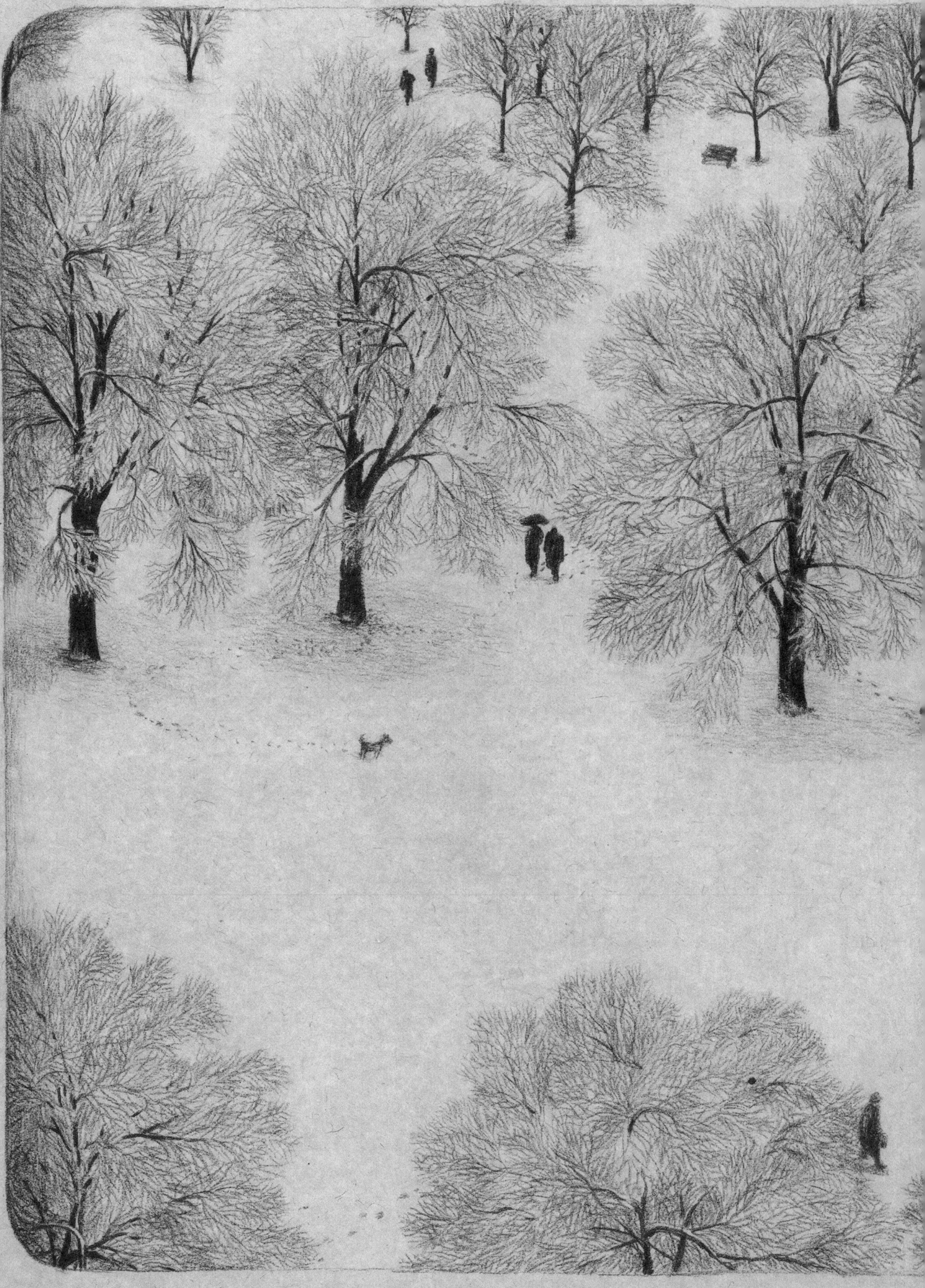

If someone could look down on us from above, they'd see that the world is full of people running about in a hurry, sweating and very tired, and their lost souls . . .

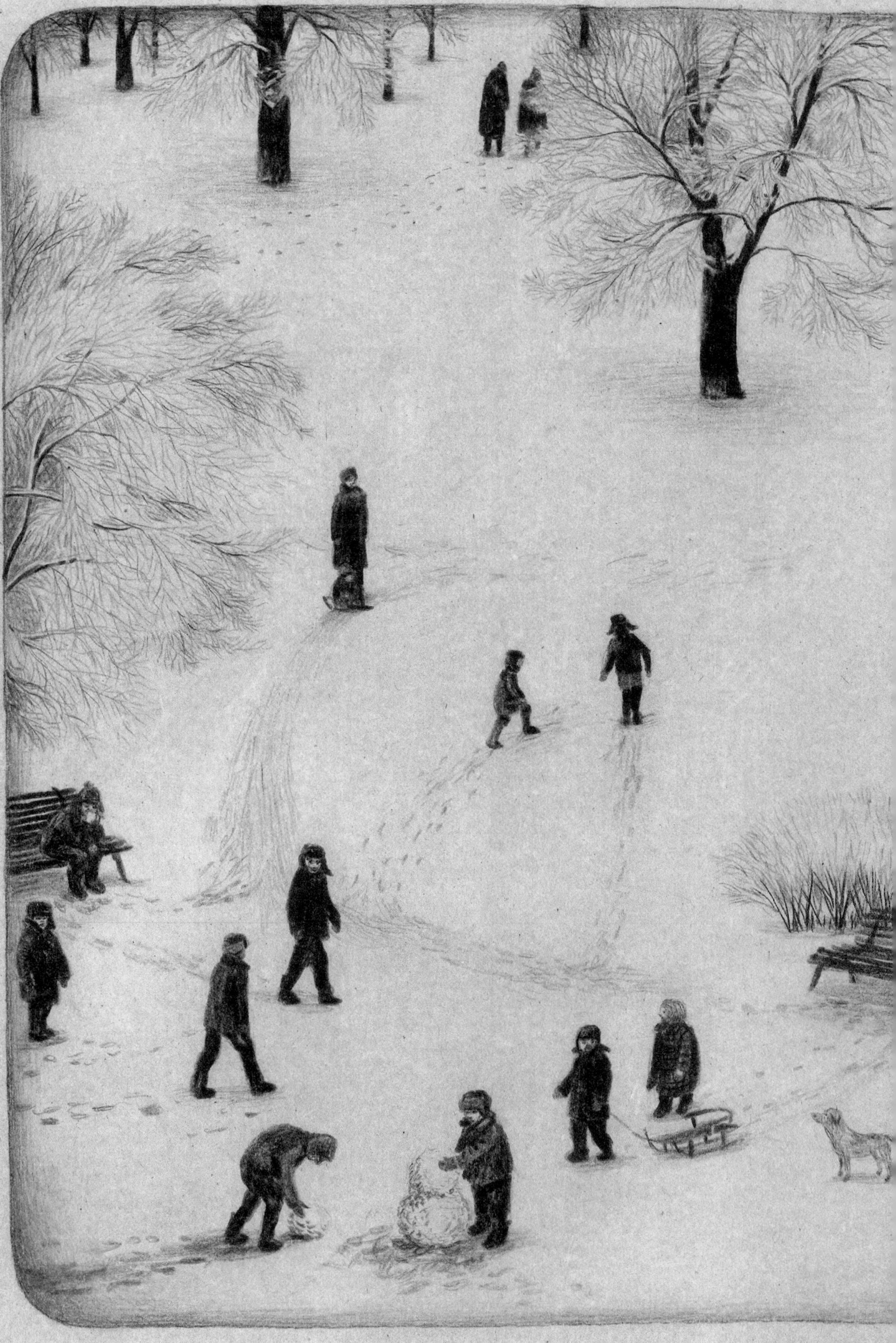

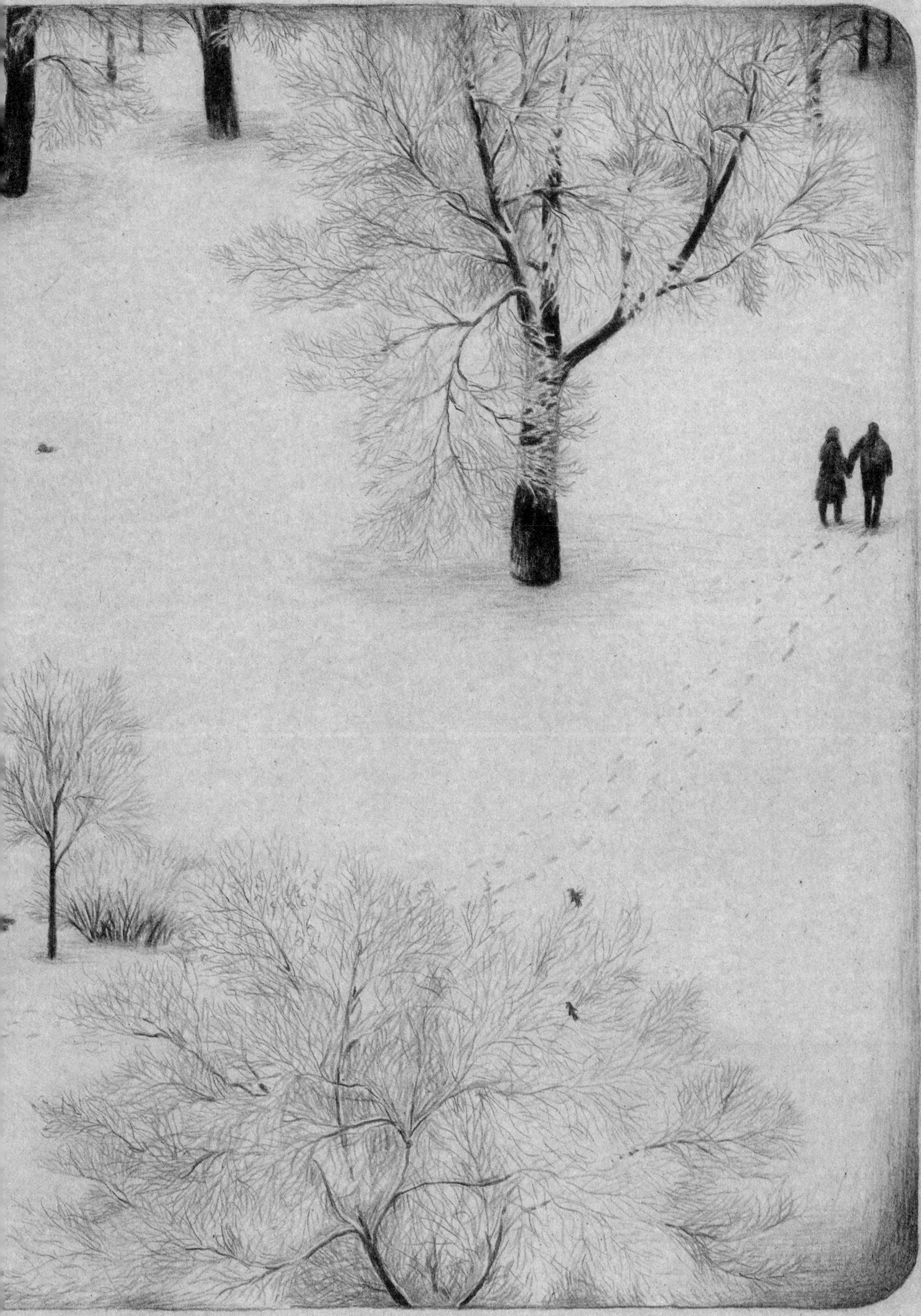

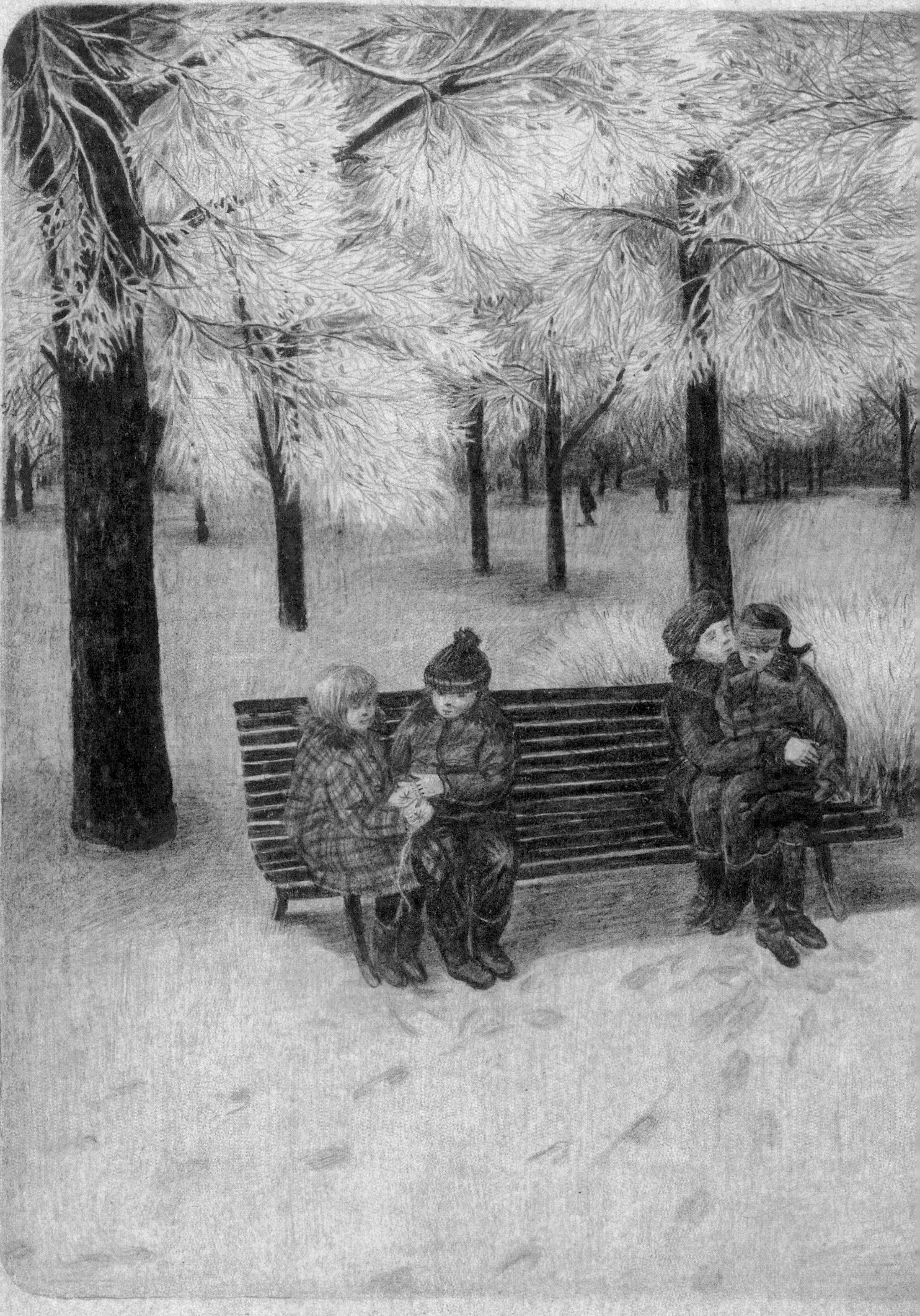

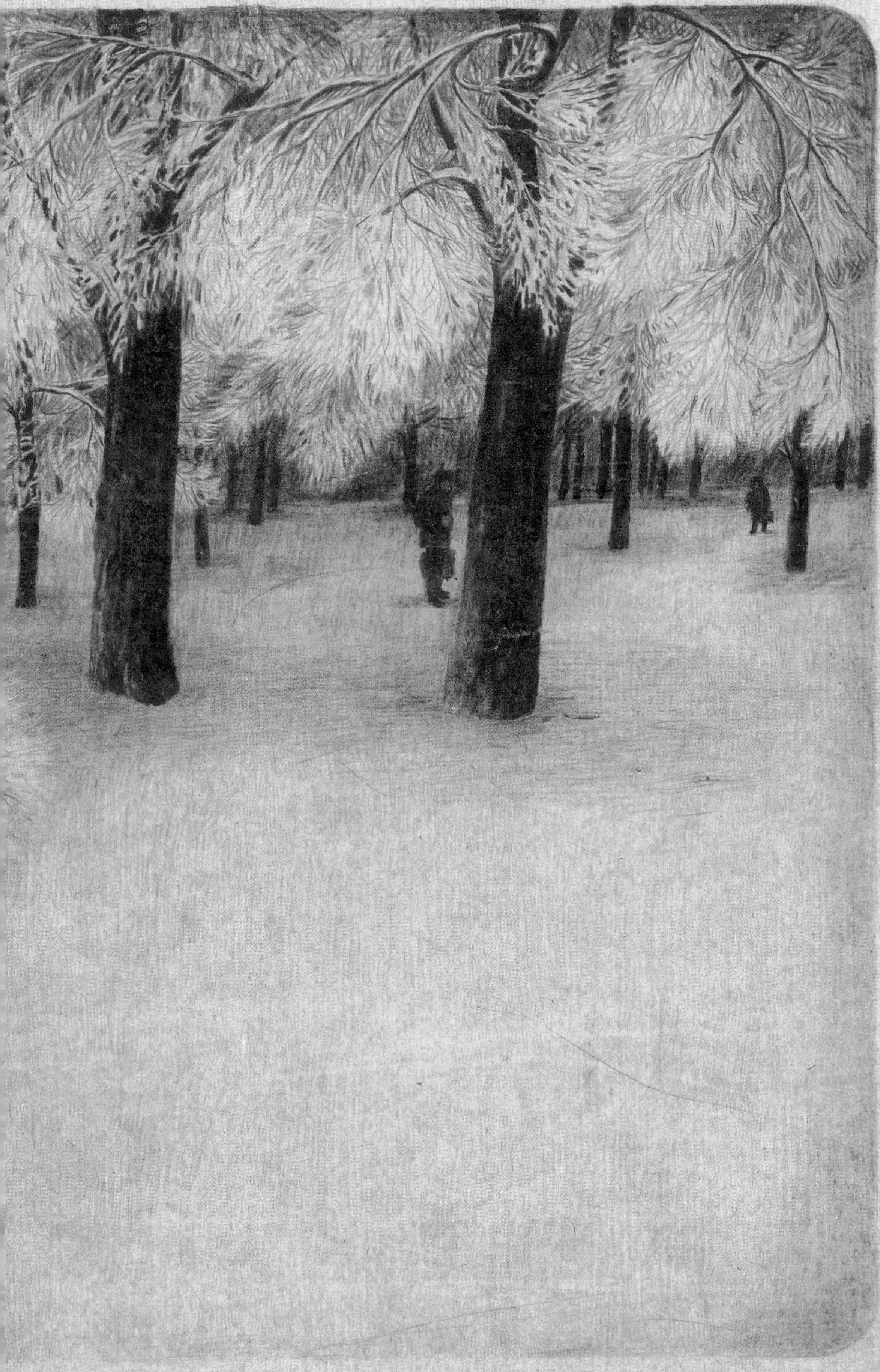

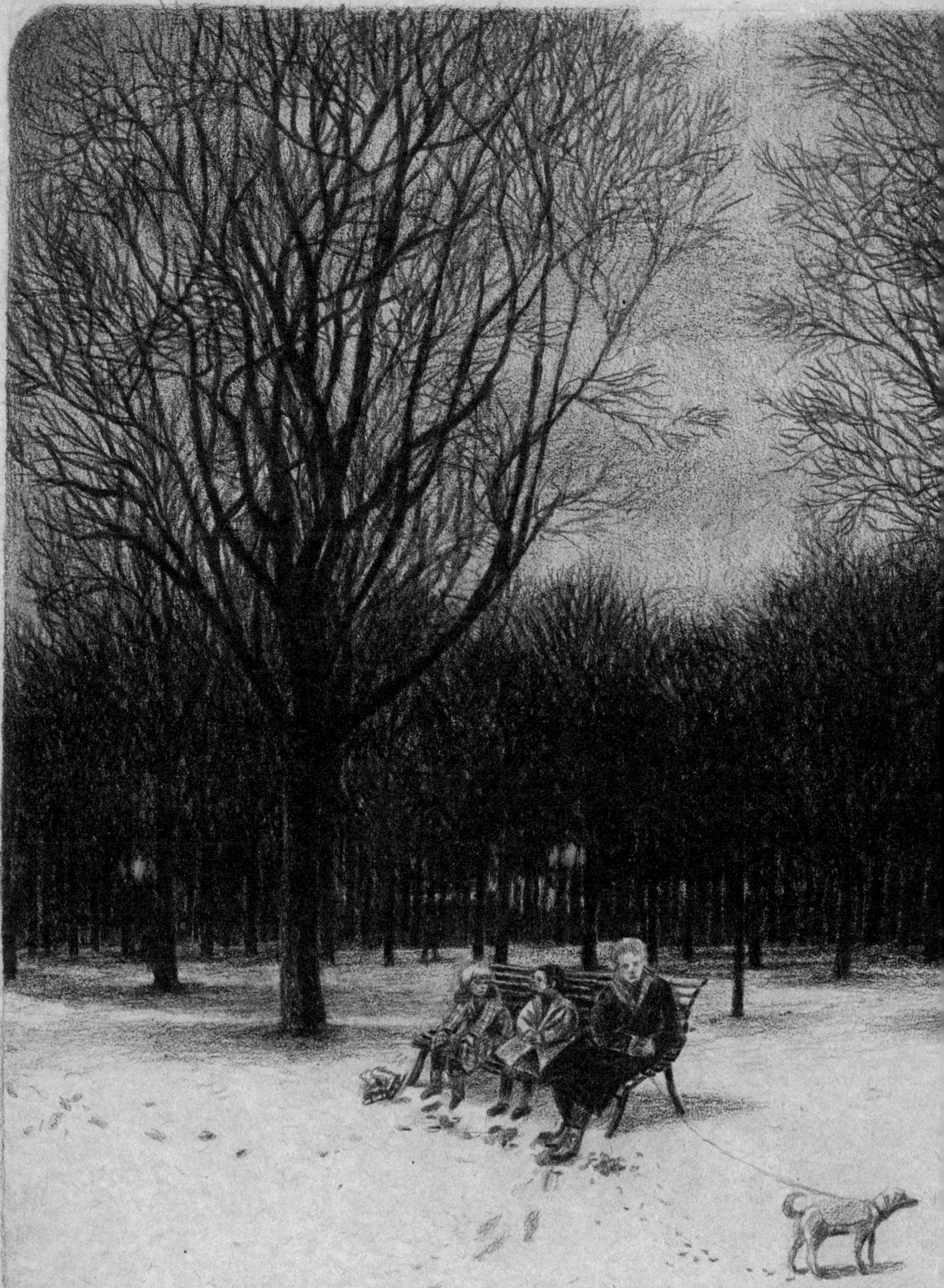

Olga Tokarczuk
Joanna Concejo

The Lost
Soul

Translated by Antonia Lloyd-Jones

Seven Stories Press

New York • Oakland • Liverpool

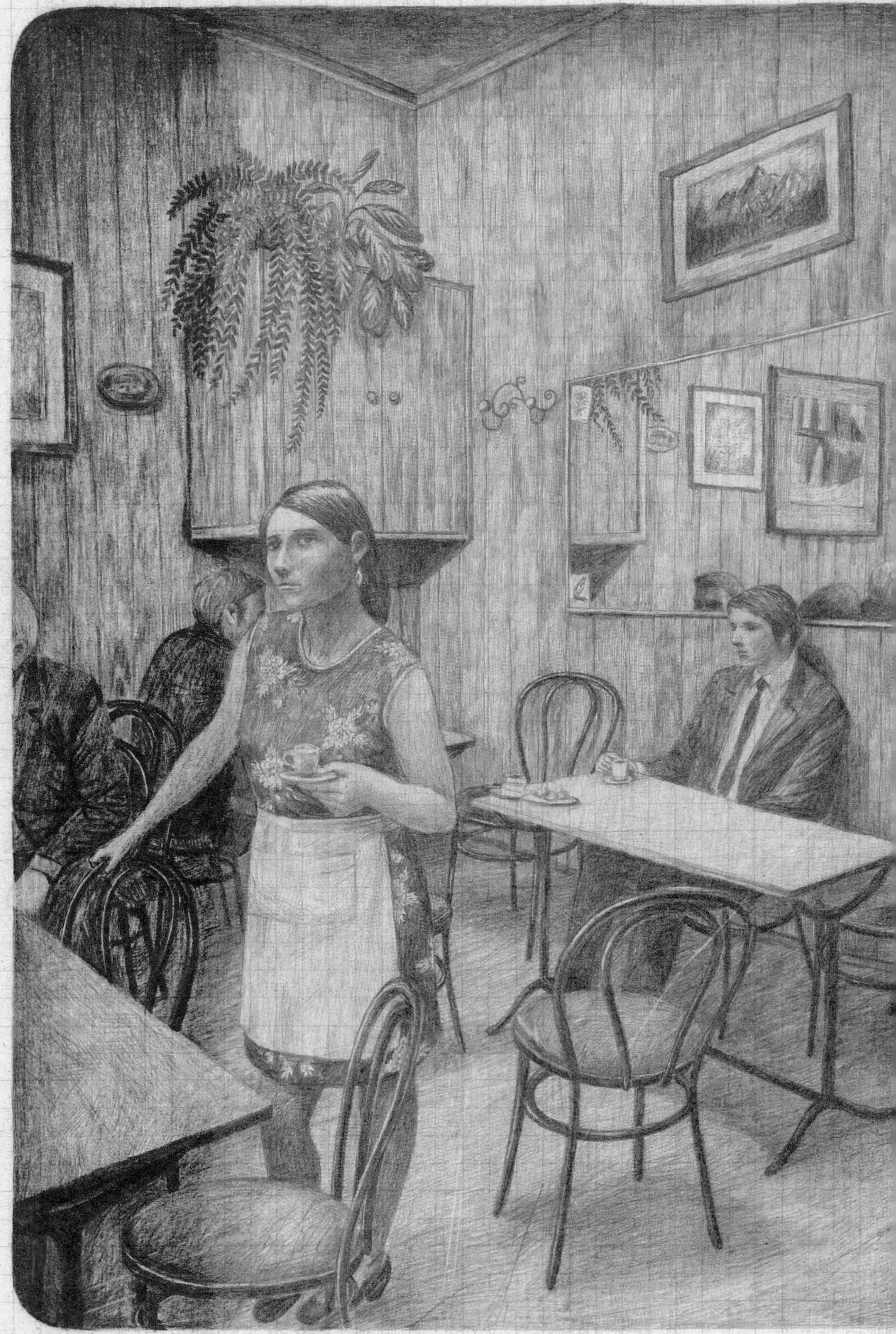

Once upon a time there was a man who worked very hard and very quickly, and who had left his soul far behind him long ago. In fact, his life was all right without his soul—he slept, ate, worked, drove a car, and even played tennis. But sometimes he felt as if the world around him were flat, as if he were moving across a smooth page in a math exercise book, entirely covered in evenly spaced squares.

Finally, during one of his many journeys, the man awoke in the middle of the night in his hotel room and felt as if he couldn't breathe. He looked out the window, but he wasn't sure what city he was in—all cities look the same through hotel windows. Nor was he sure how he came to be there or why. And unfortunately he had forgotten his own name too. It was a strange feeling—he had no idea how he was going to find himself again. So he just kept very quiet. He didn't say a word to himself all morning, and that made him feel extremely lonely, as if there were no one inside his body anymore. When he stood before the mirror in the bathroom he saw himself as a blurred streak. For a while he thought his name might be Andrew, but all of a sudden he felt sure it was Matthew. Finally, in a state of panic, he dug his passport out of the bottom of his suitcase and saw that his name was John.

The next day he went to see a wise old doctor, and this is what she told him:

"If someone could look down on us from above, they'd see that the world is full of people running about in a hurry, sweating and very tired, and their lost souls, always left behind, unable to keep up with their owners. The result is great confusion as the souls lose their heads and the people cease to have hearts. The souls know they've lost their owners, but most of the people don't realize that they've lost their own souls."

John was alarmed by this diagnosis.

"How on earth is it possible? Have I lost my own soul too?" he asked.

The wise doctor answered:

"It happens because souls move at a much slower speed than bodies. They were born at the dawn of time, just after the Big Bang, when the cosmos wasn't yet in such a rush, so it could still see itself in the mirror. You must find a place of your own, sit there quietly, and wait for your soul. Right now it's sure to be wherever you were two or three years ago. So the waiting might take a while. I can't think of any other cure for you."

So that's exactly what the man called John did. He found himself a small cottage at the edge of the city and sat there day after day, waiting. He didn't do anything else. This went on for many days, weeks, and months. John's hair grew long, and his beard came down to his waist.

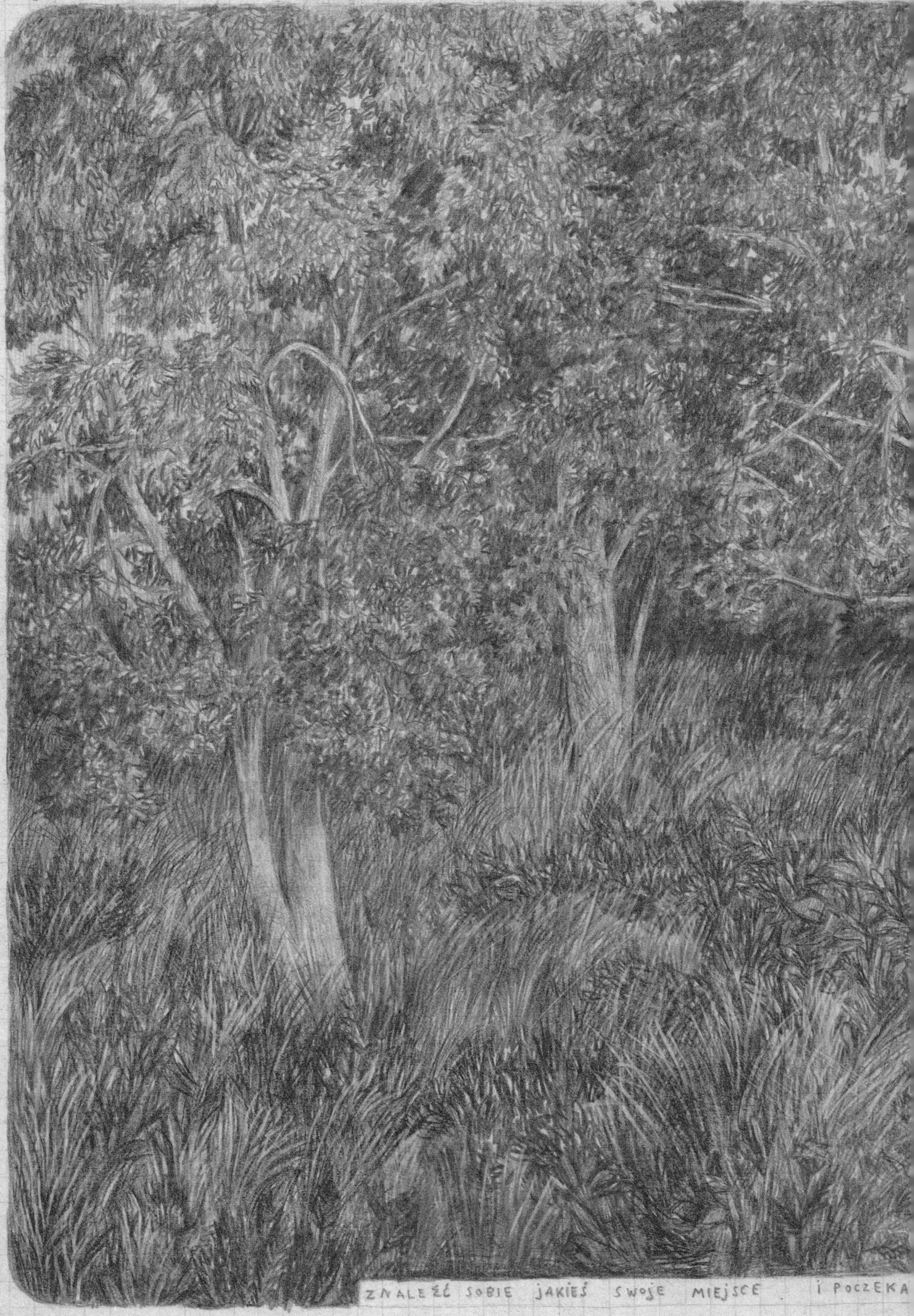
ZNALEŹĆ SOBIE JAKIEŚ SWOJE MIEJSCE I POCZEKA

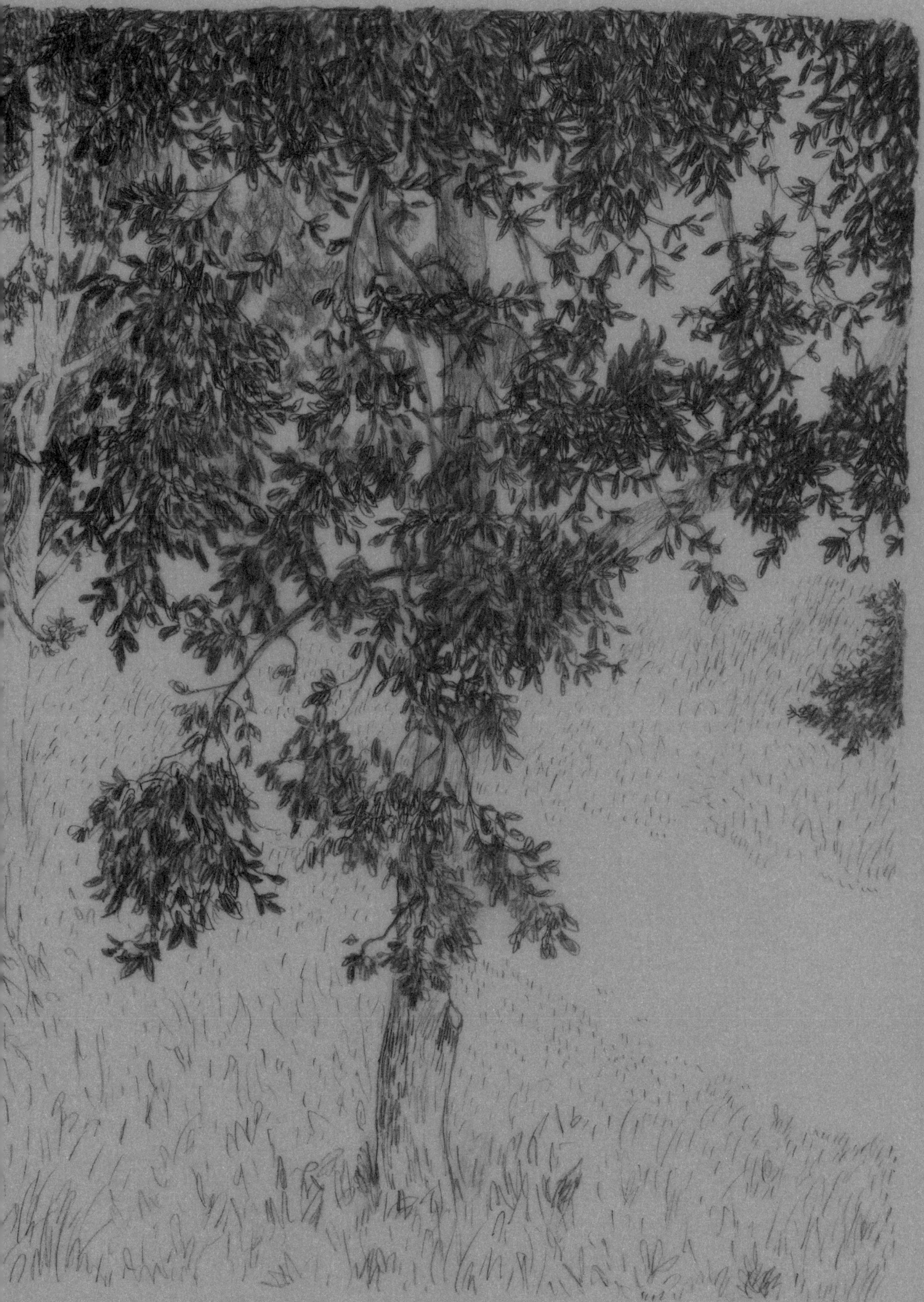

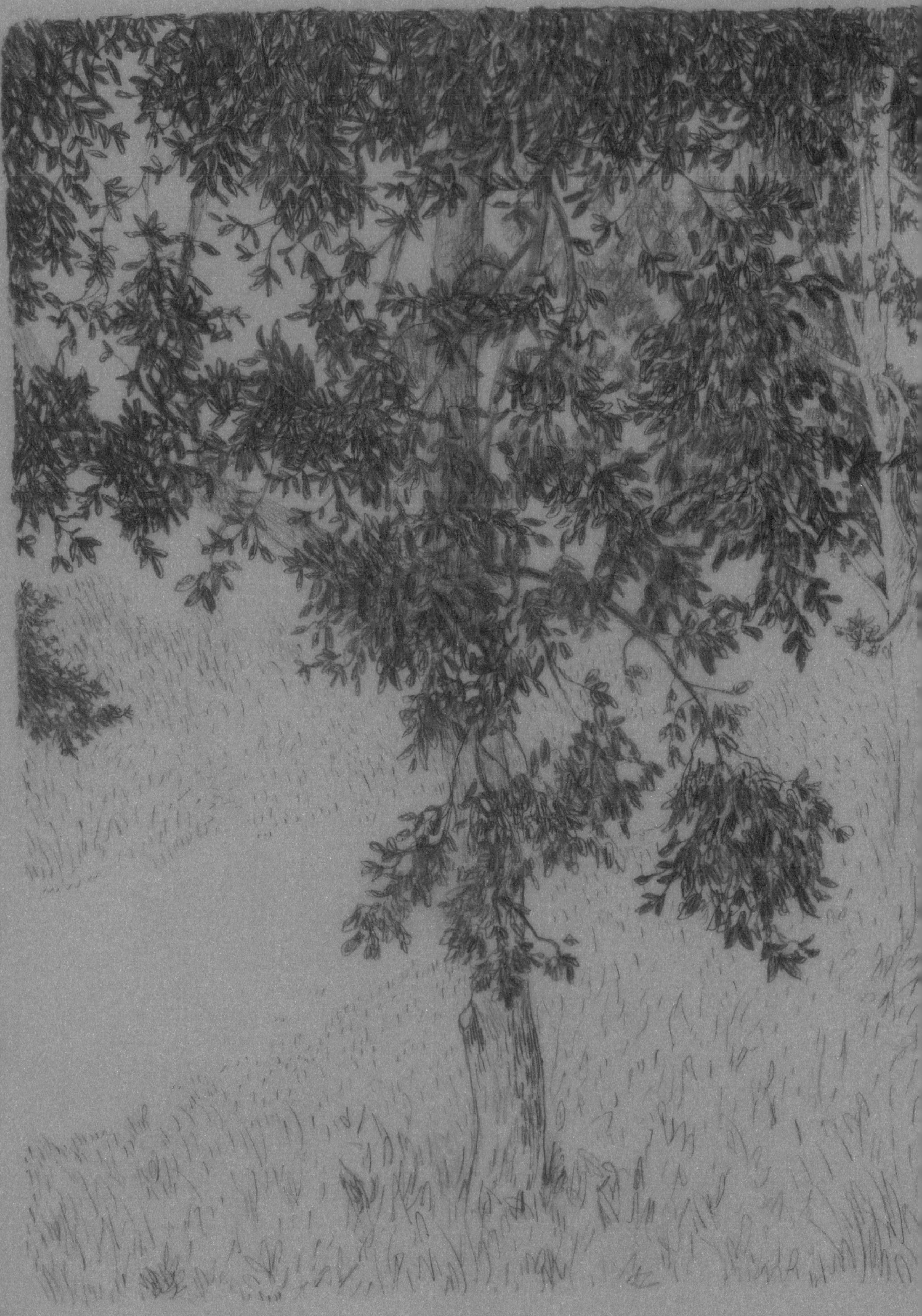

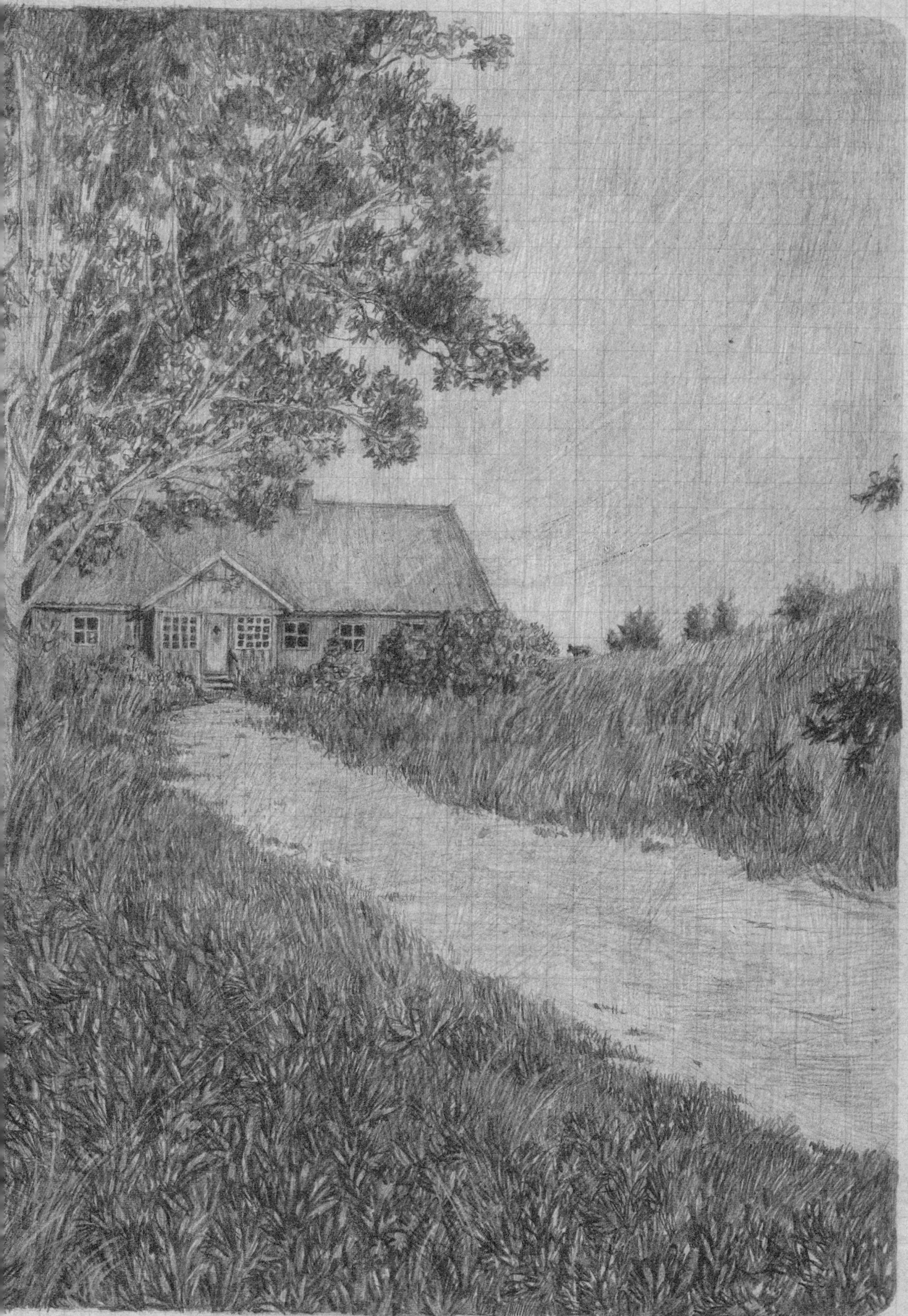

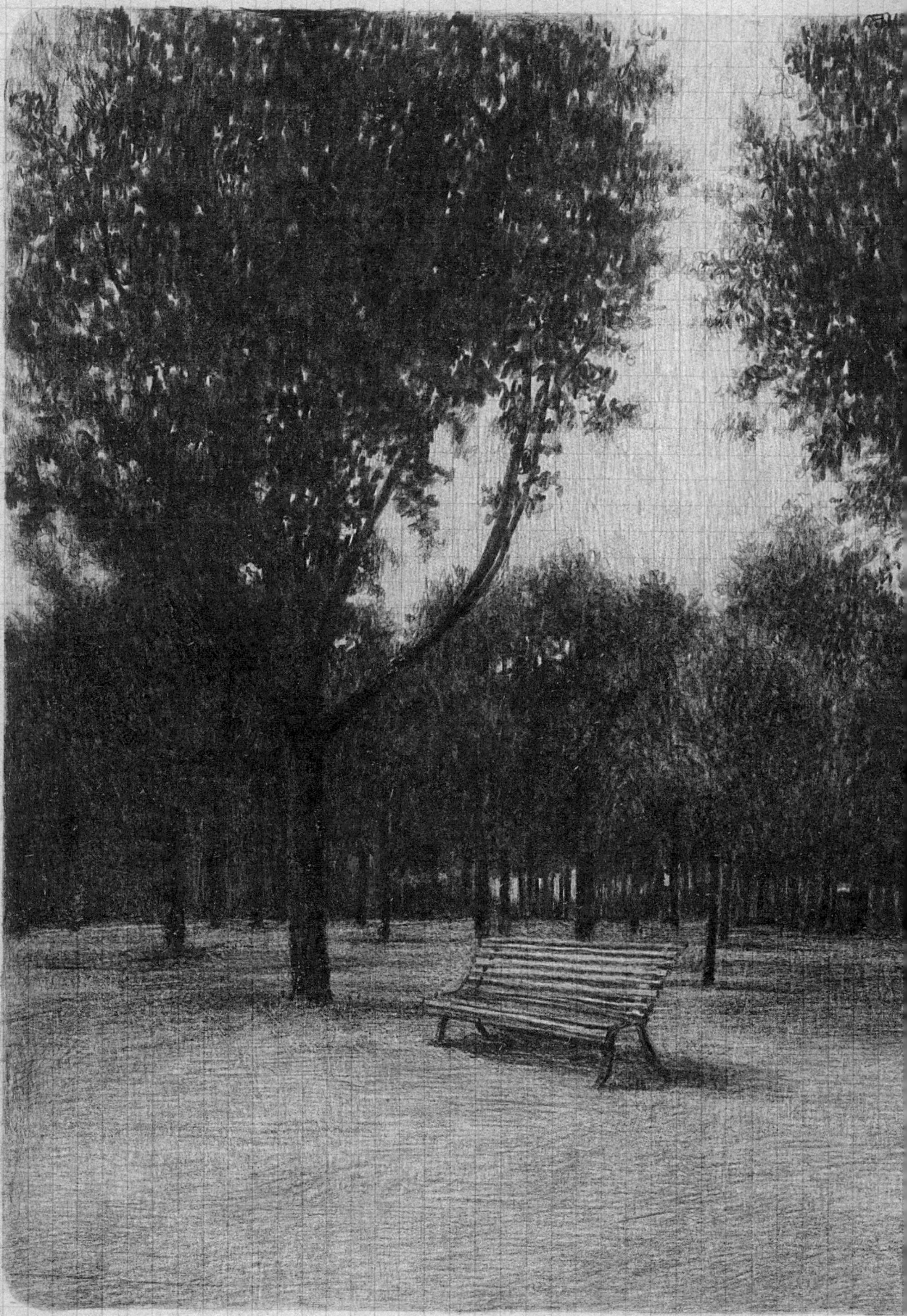

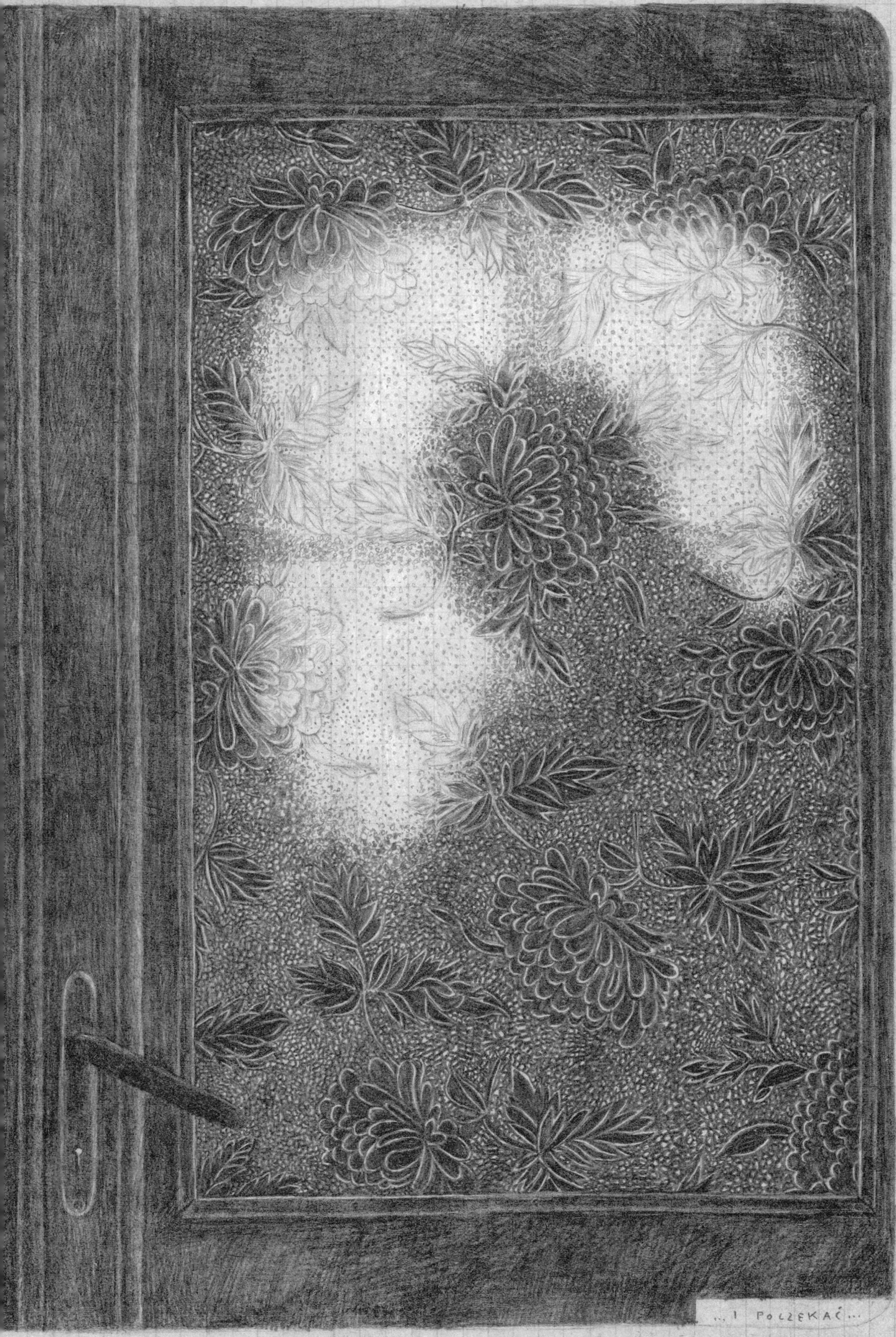

...I POCZEKAĆ...

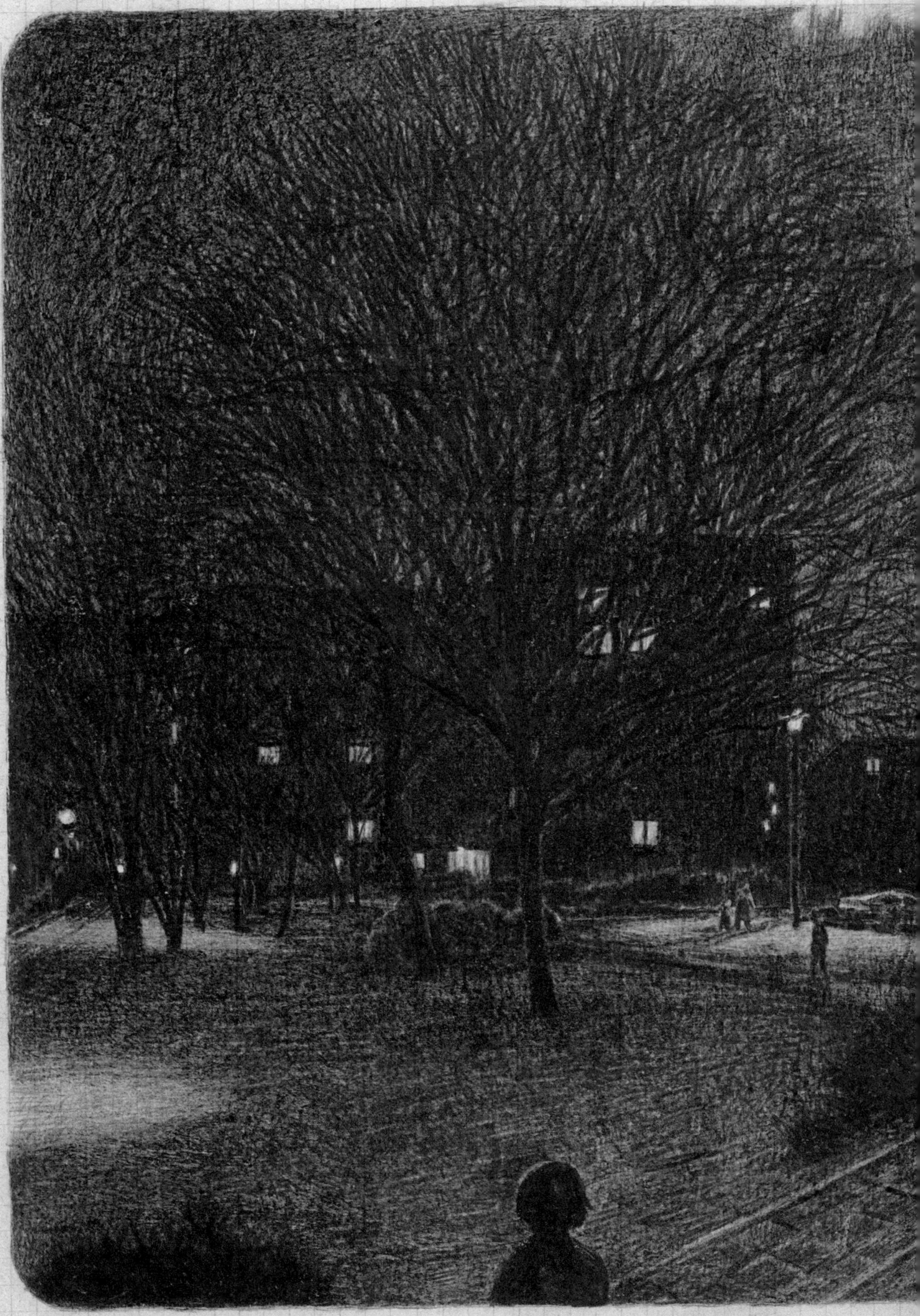

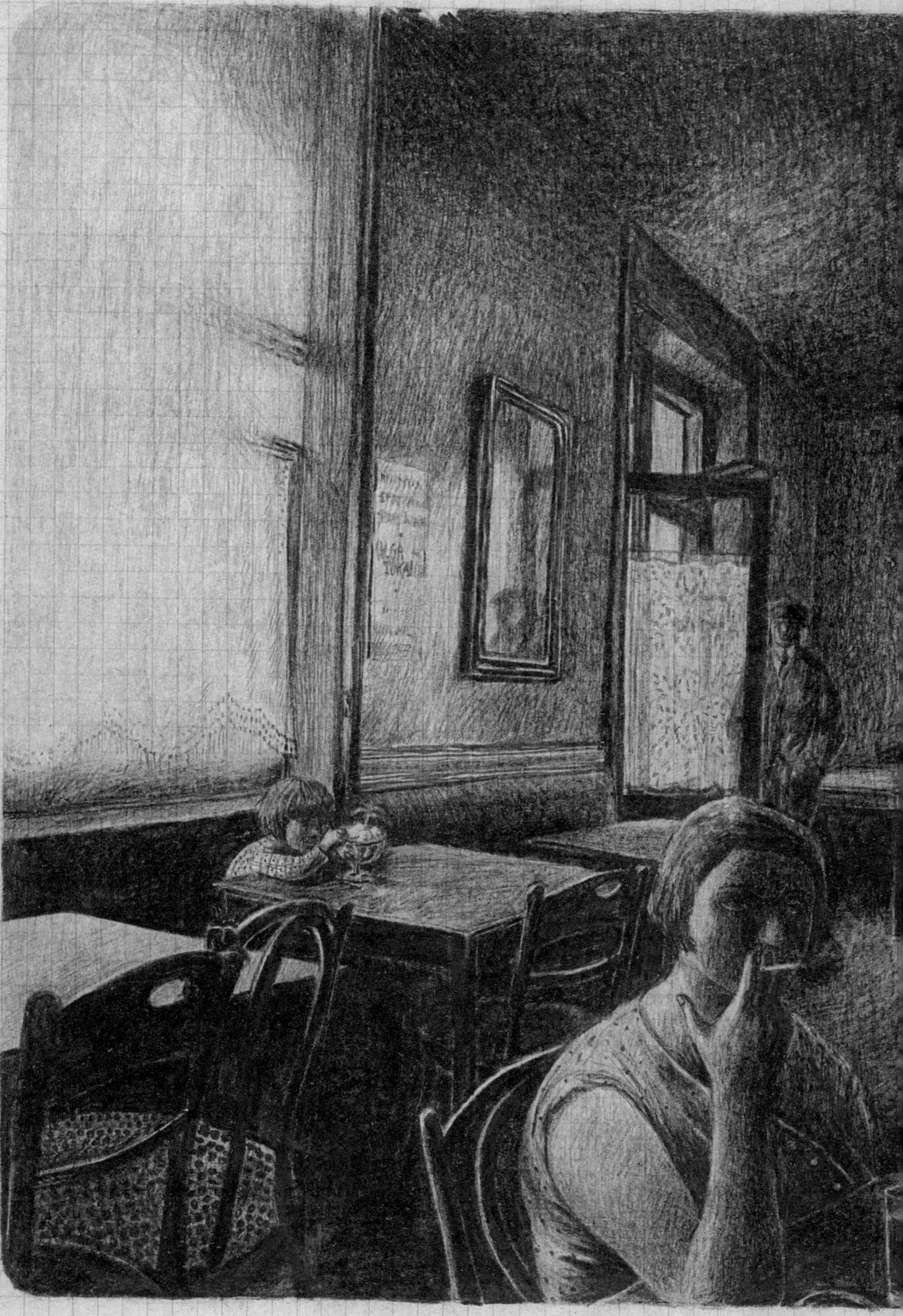

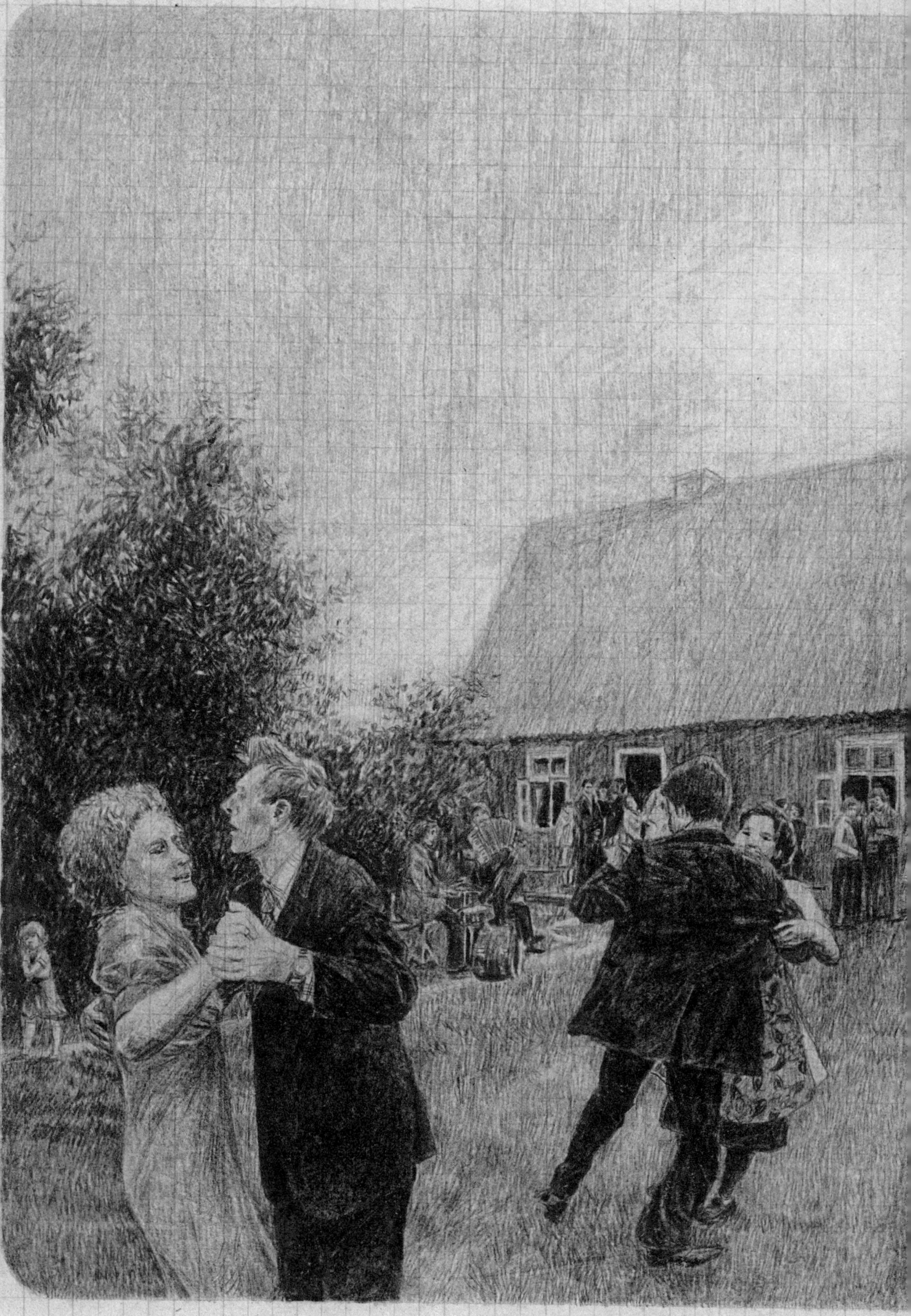

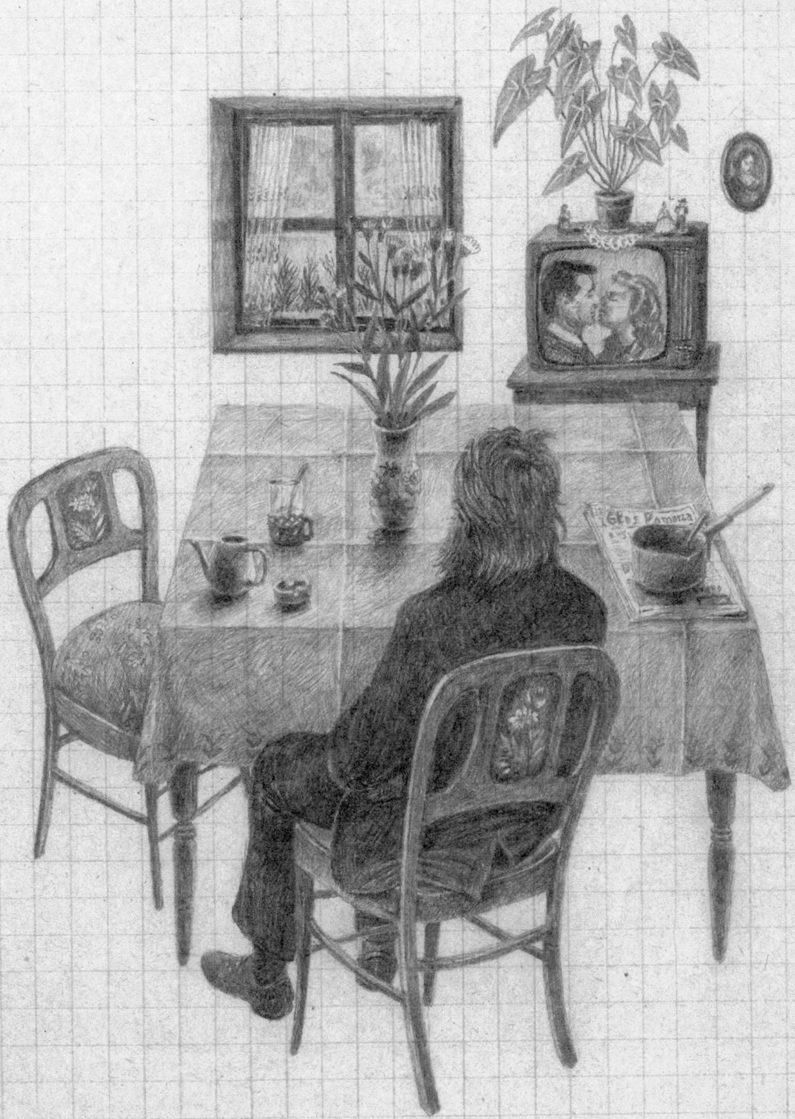
Głos Pomorza

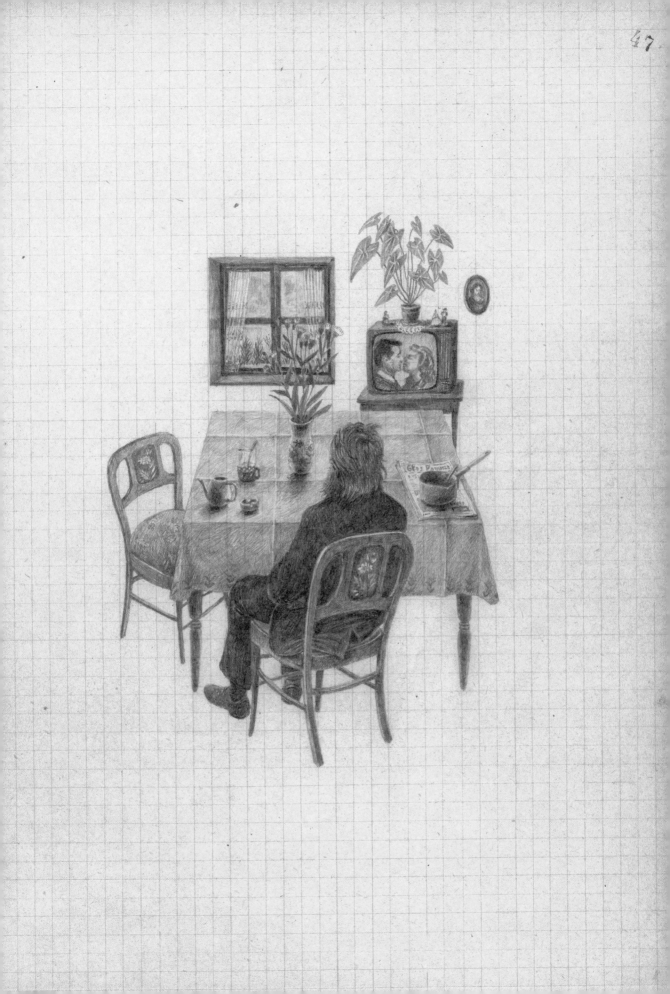

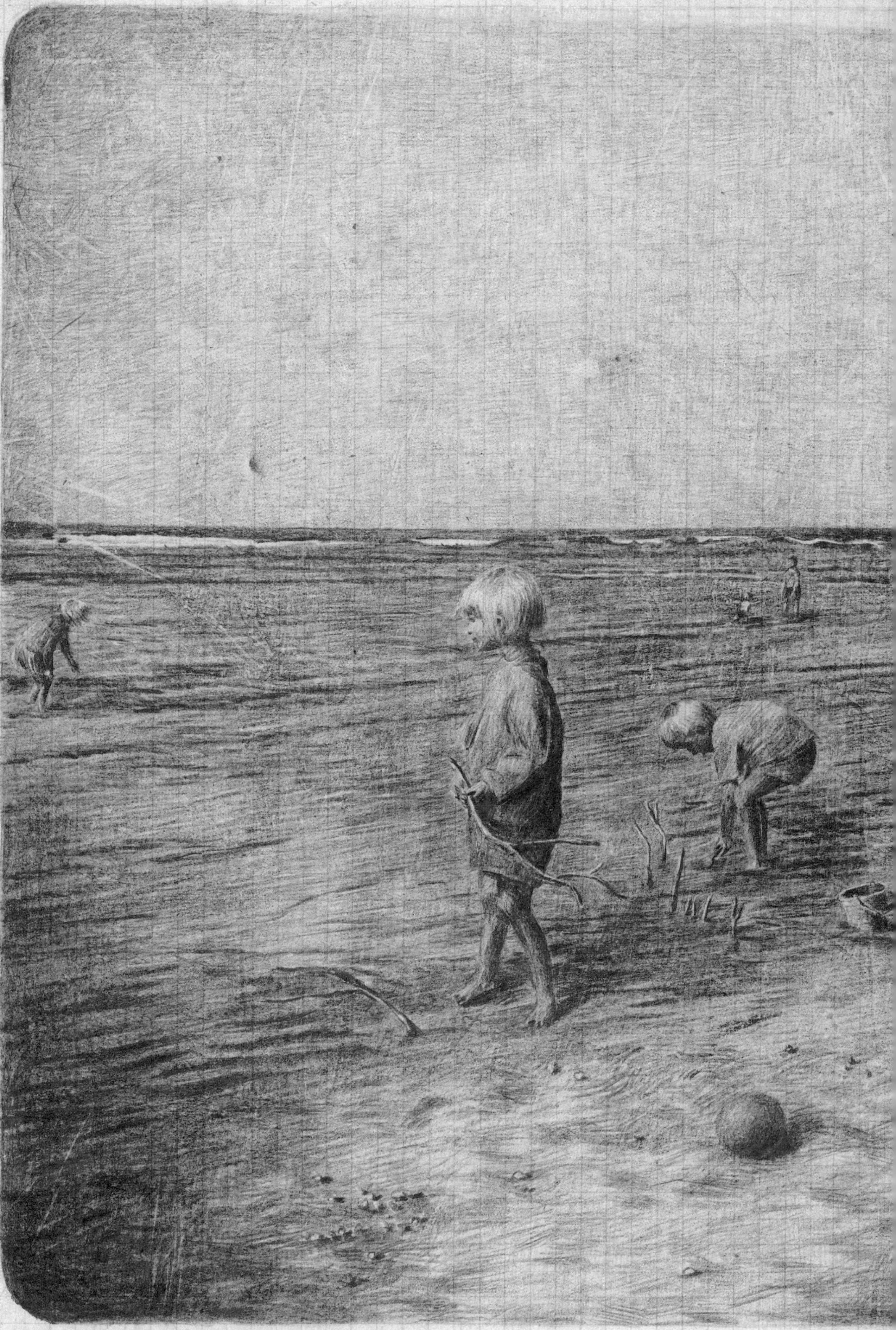

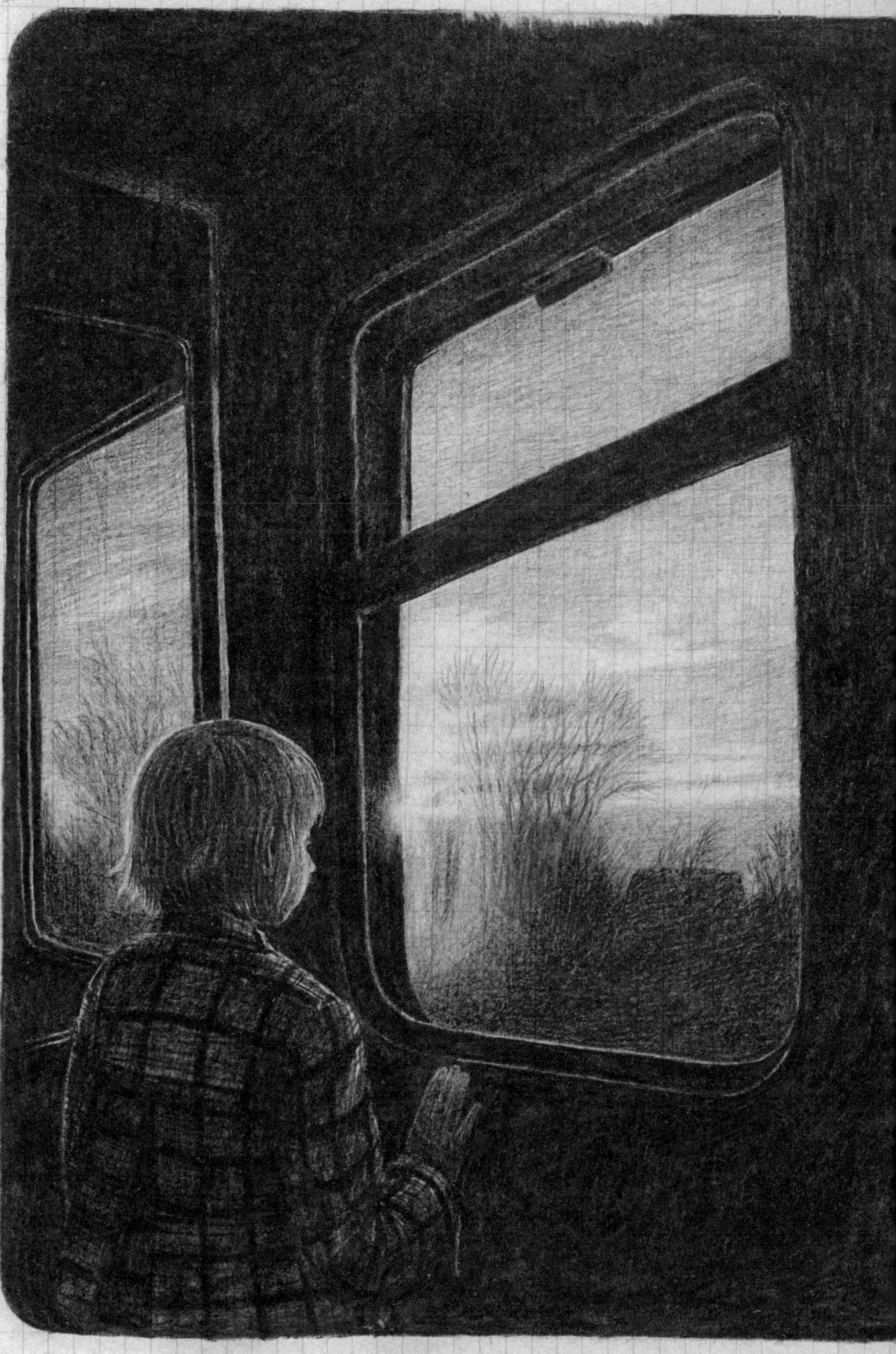

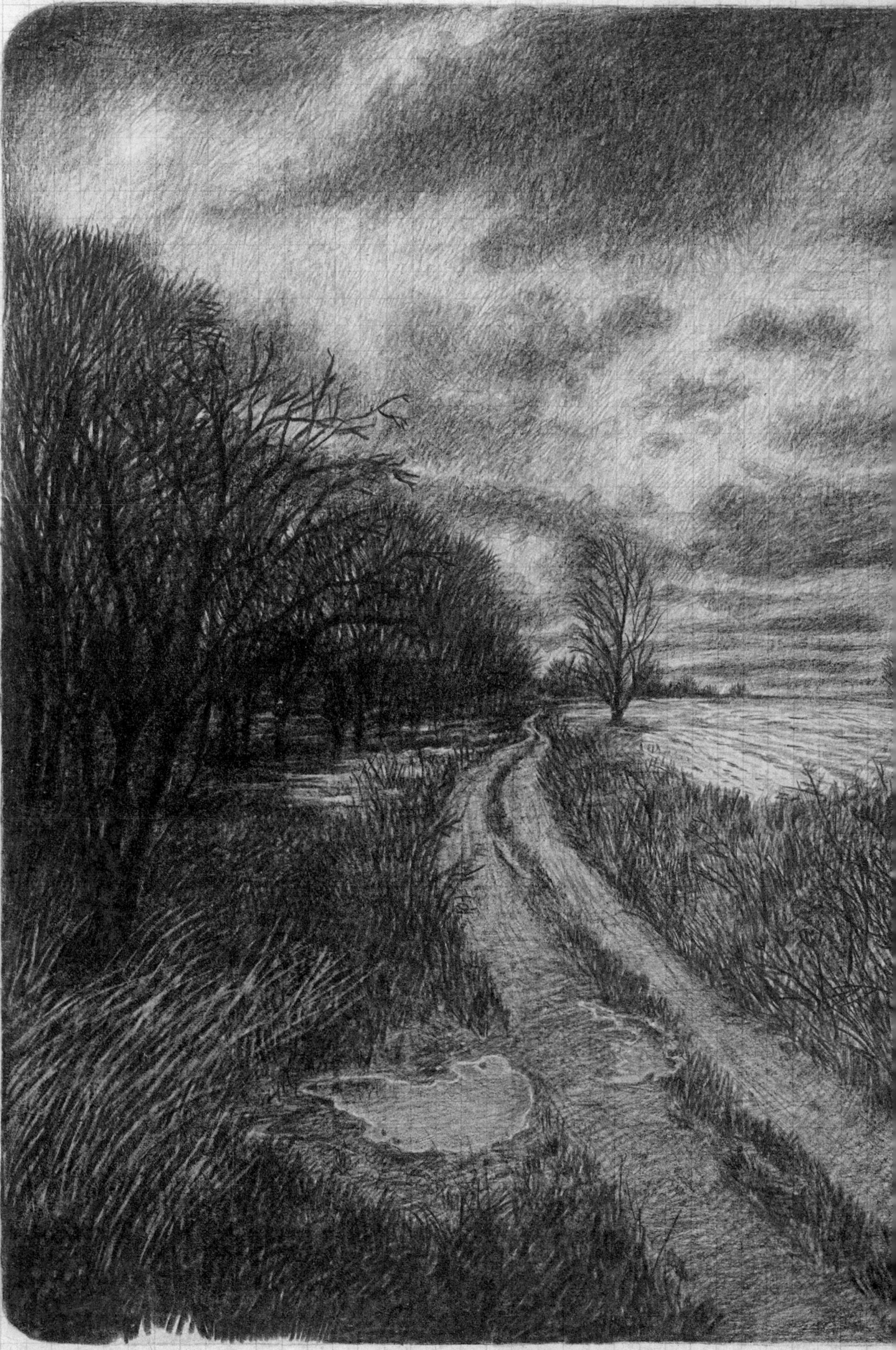

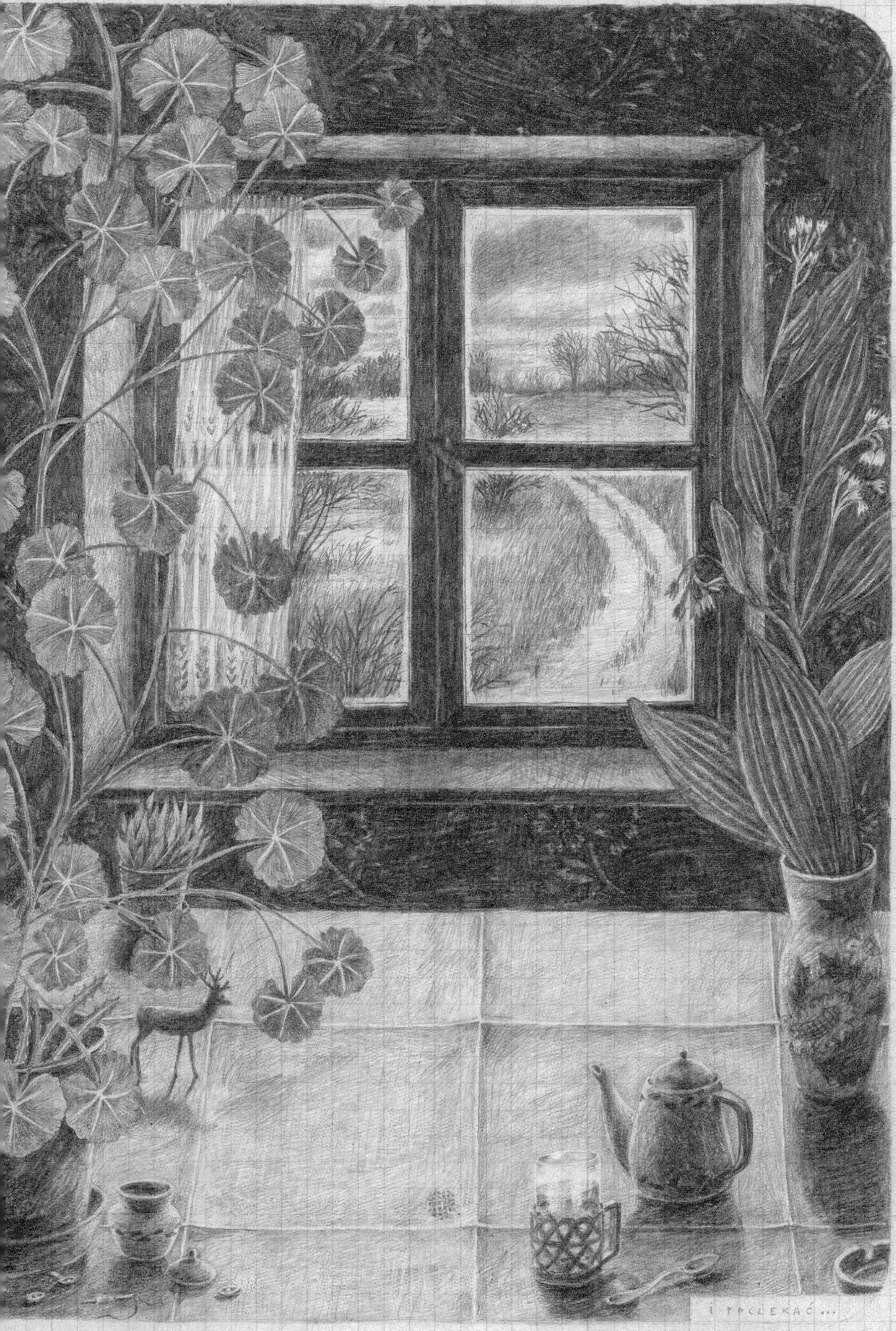

I POCZEKAĆ...

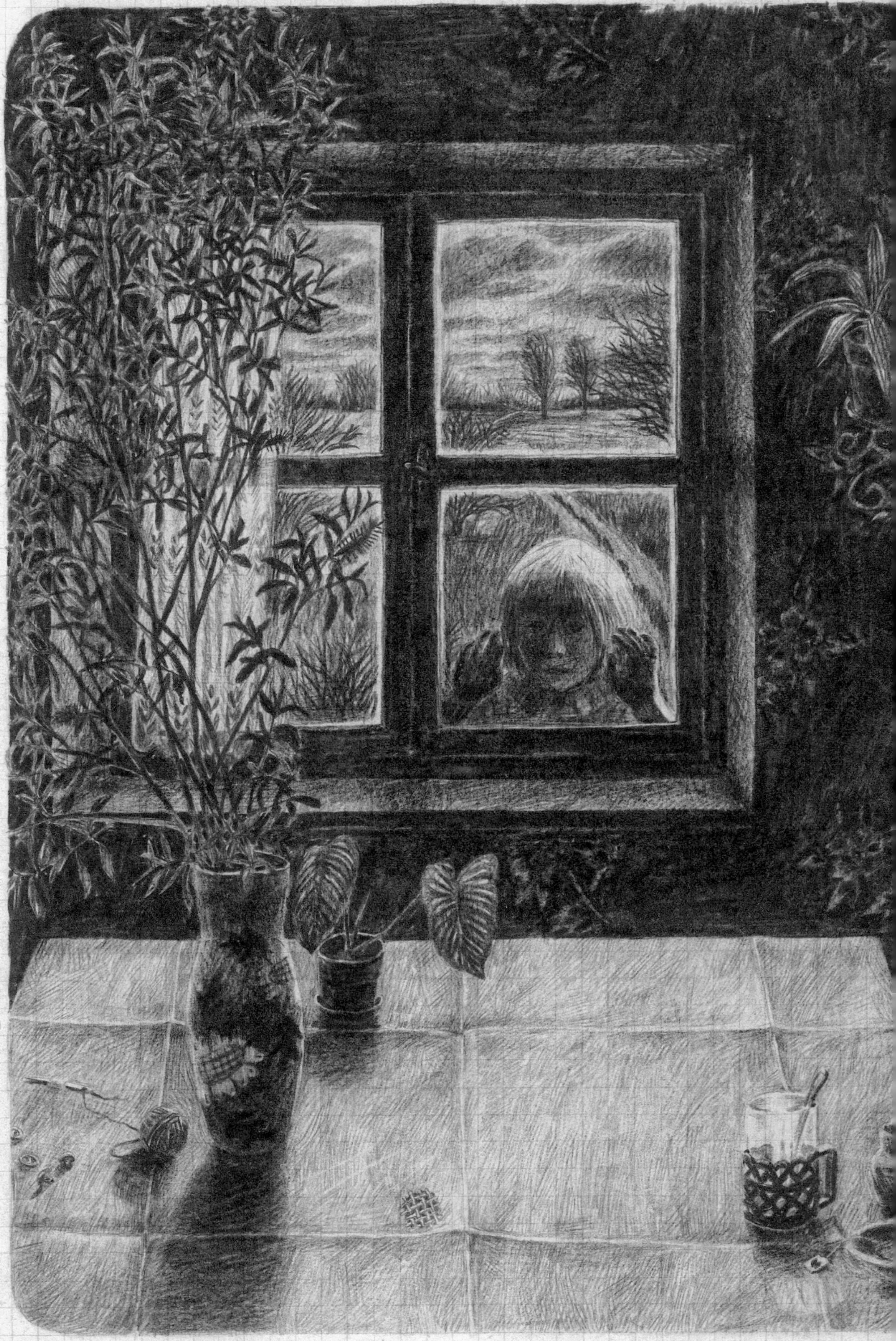

Until one afternoon someone knocked at the door, and there stood his lost soul—tired, dirty, and scratched.

"At last!" it said breathlessly.

Until one afternoon someone knocked at the door, and there stood his lost soul—tired, dirty, and scratched.

"At last!" it said breathlessly.

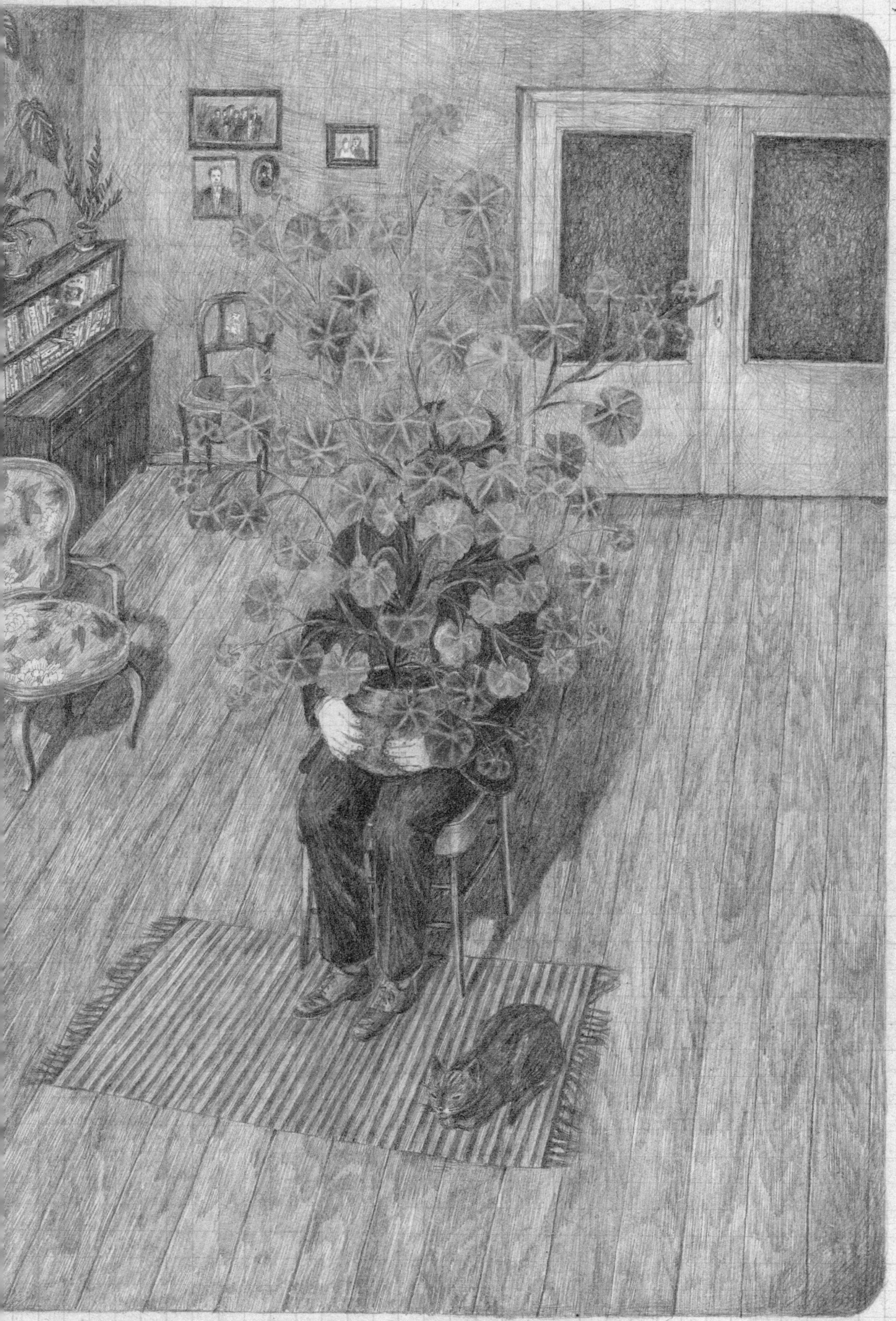

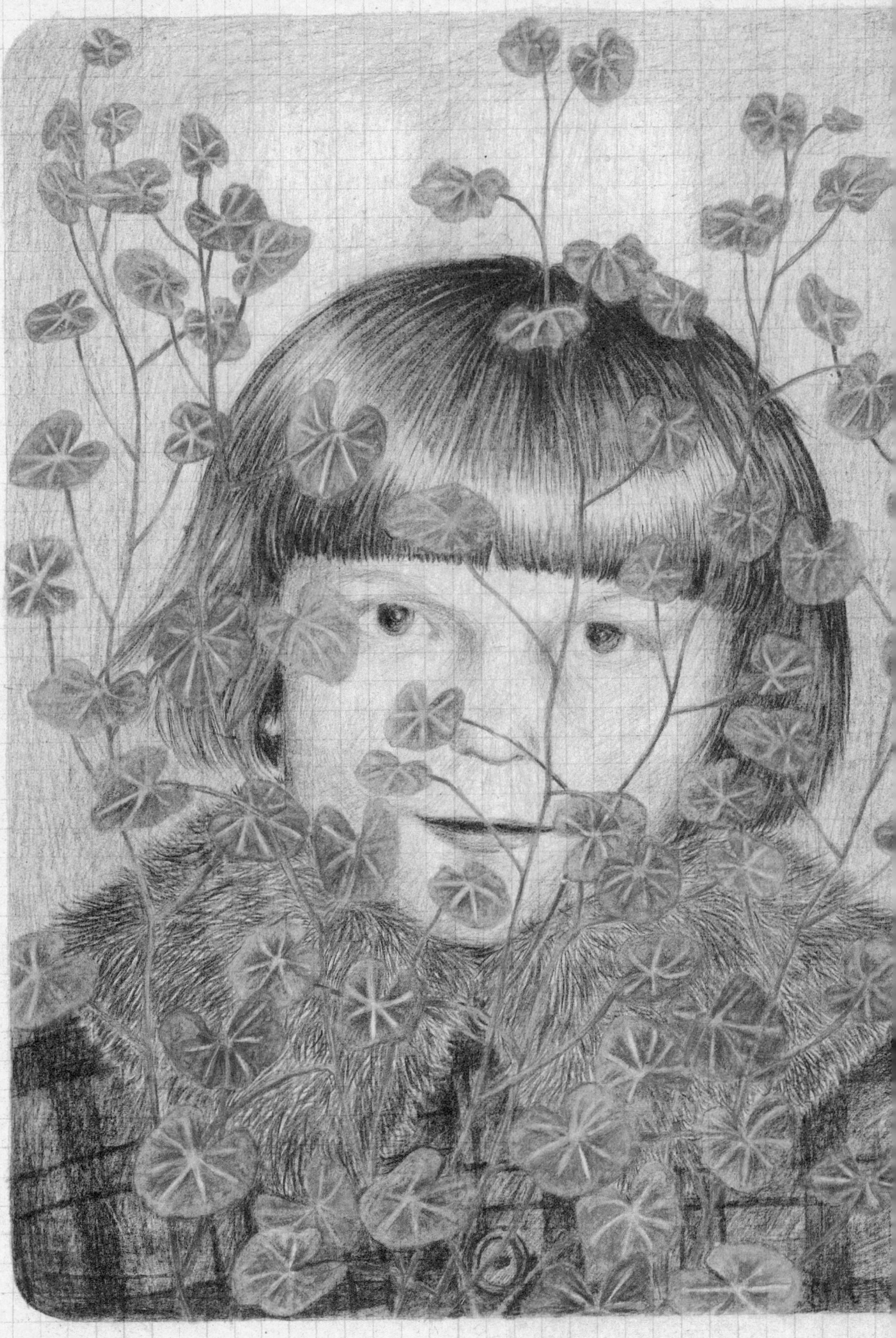

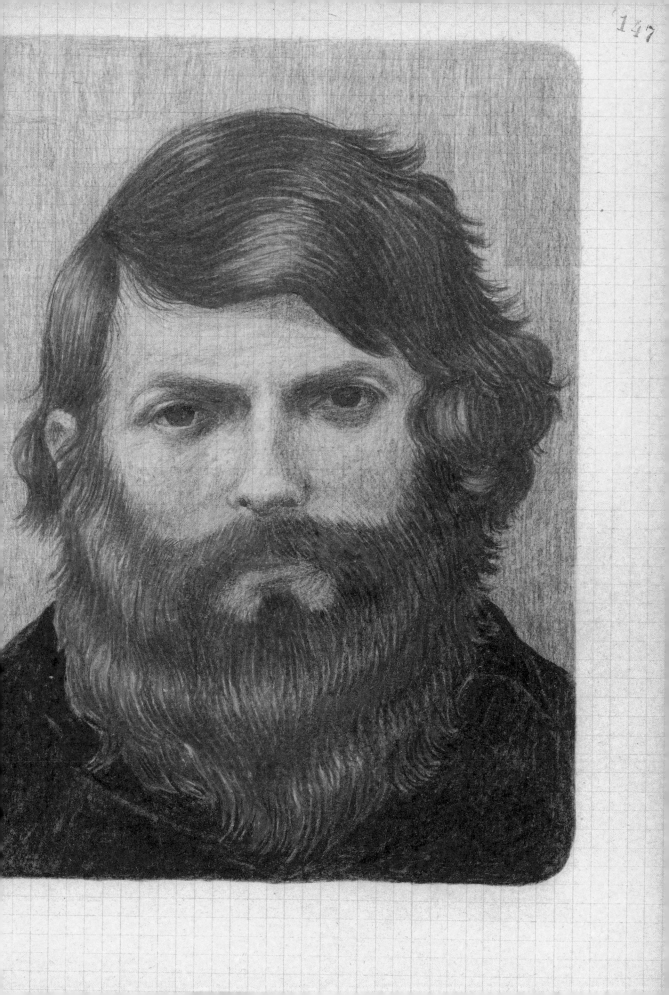

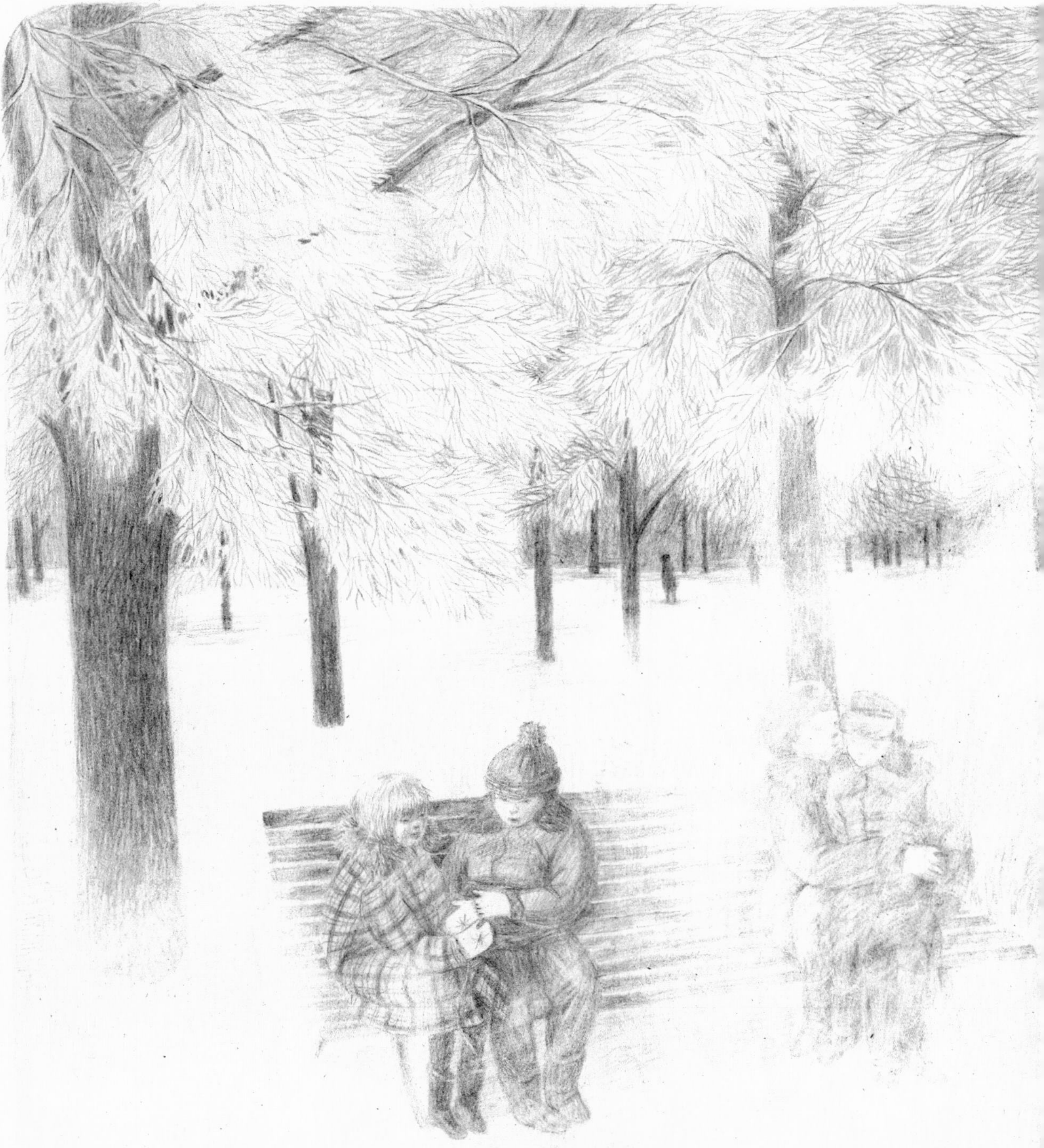

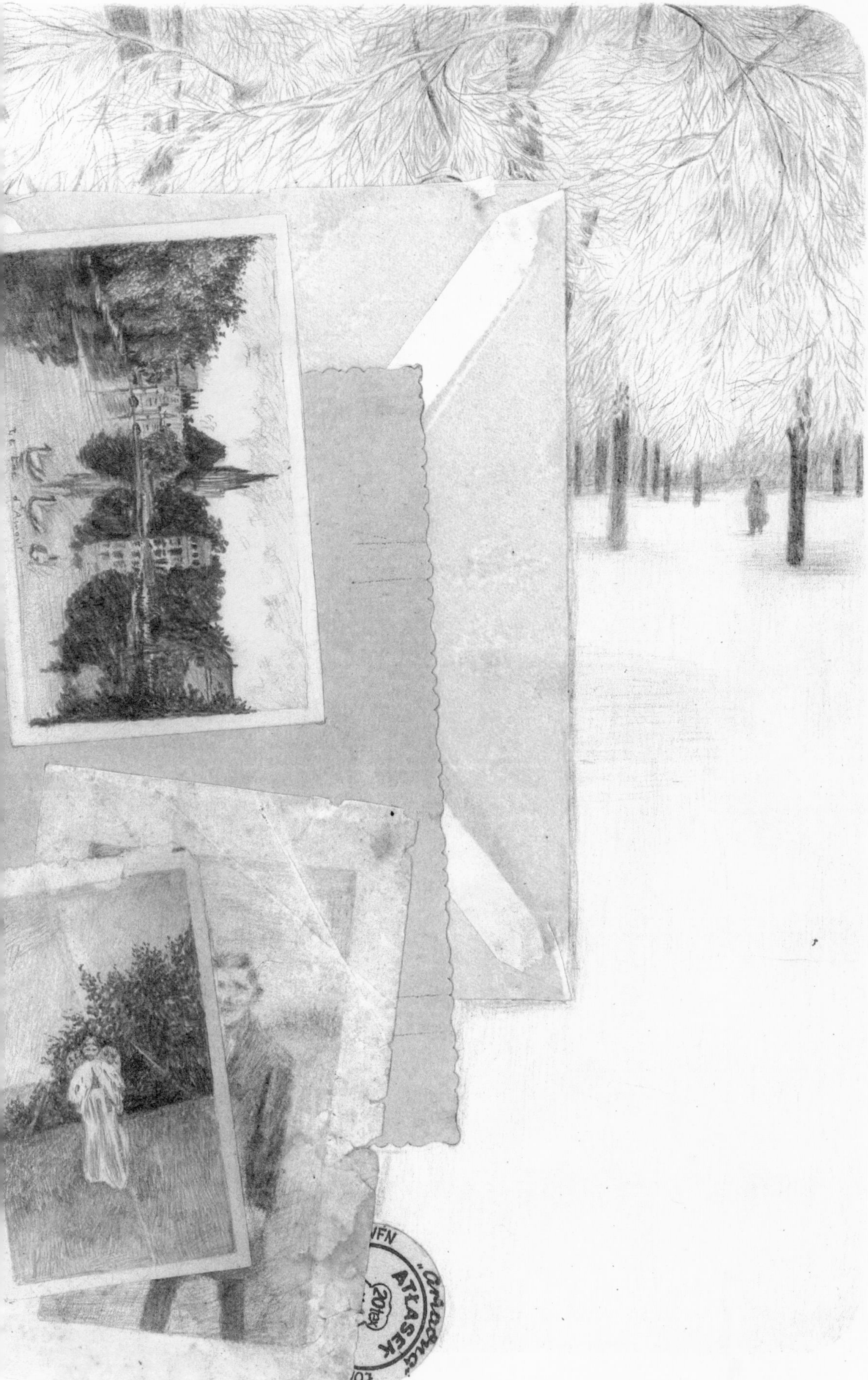

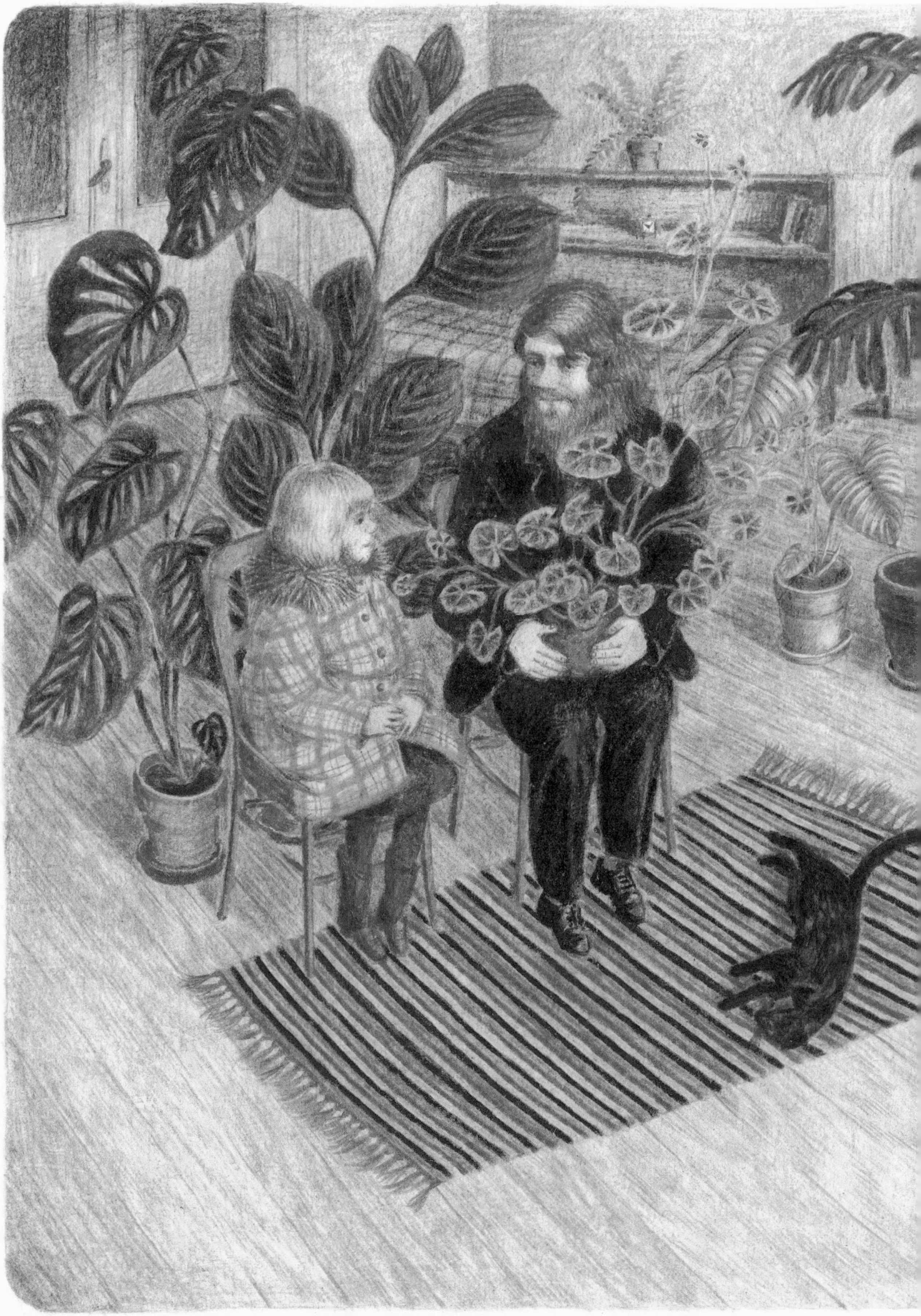

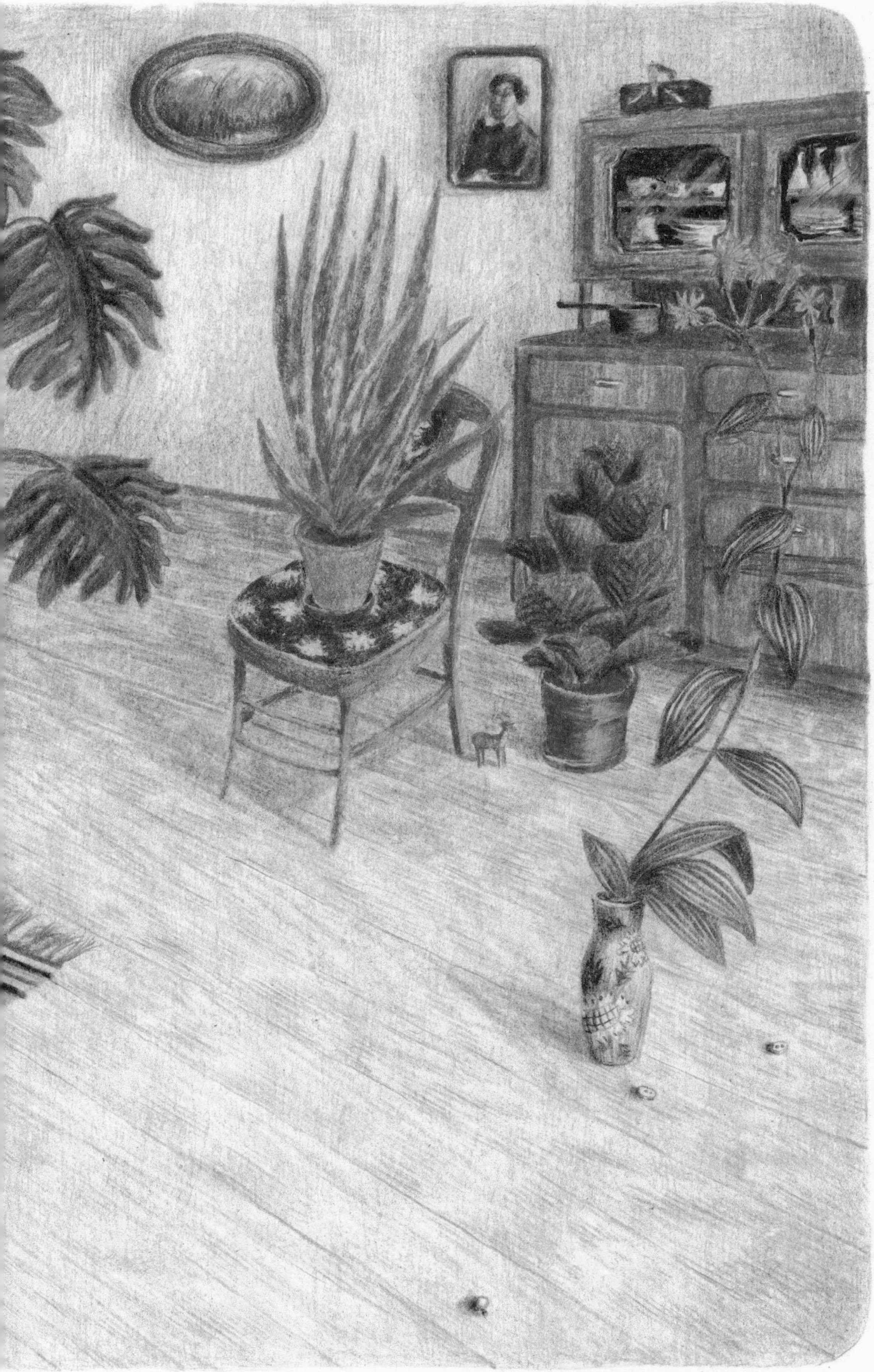

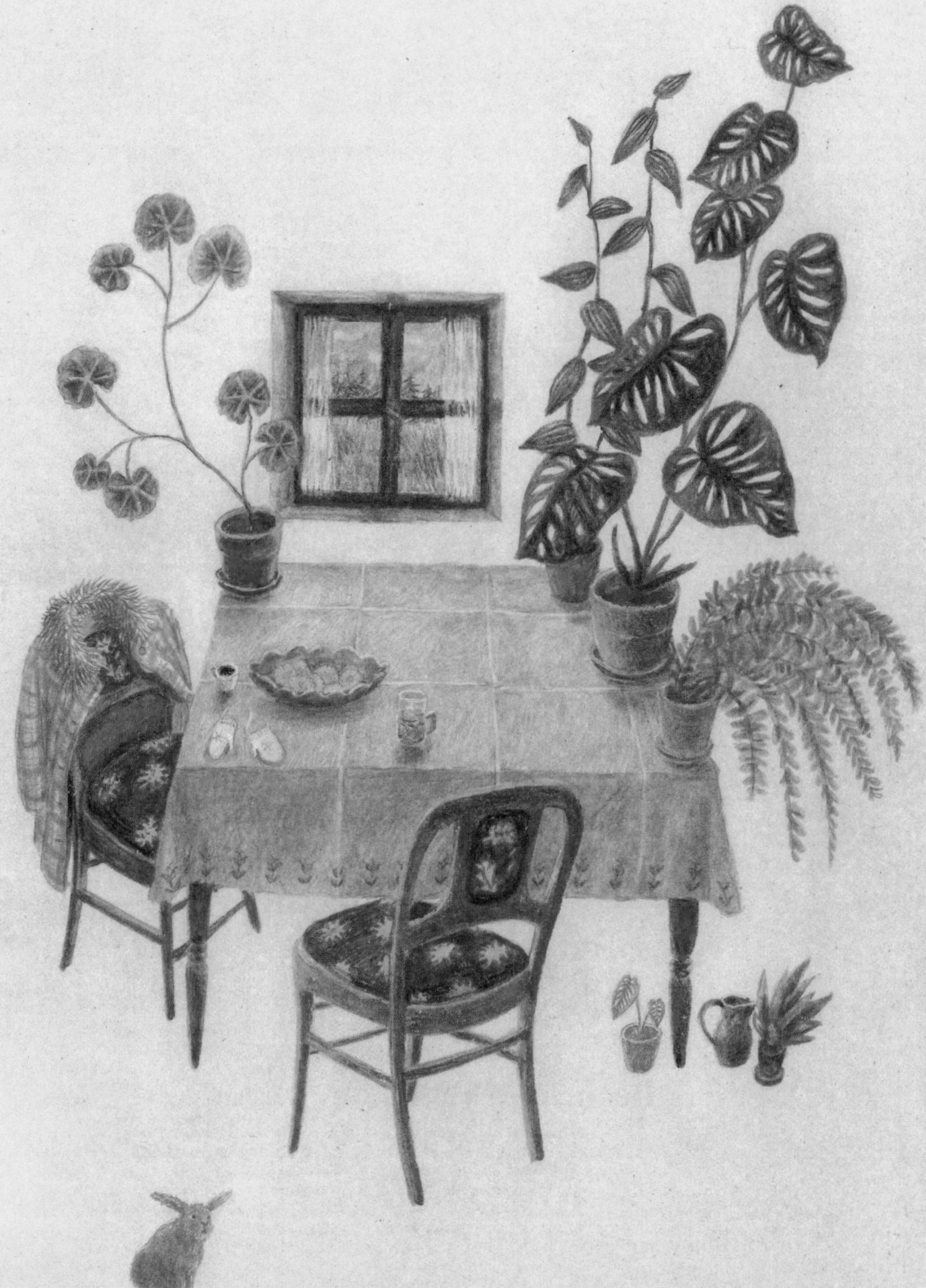

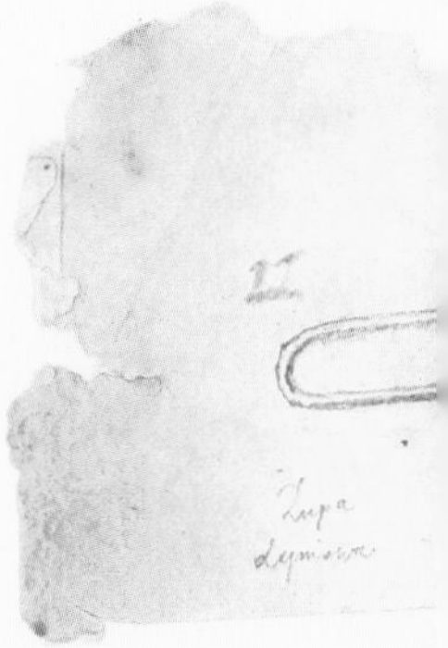

From then on they lived happily ever after, and John was very careful not to do anything too fast, so that his soul could always keep up with him. He did another thing too—he buried all his watches and suitcases in the garden. The watches grew into beautiful flowers that looked like bells, in various colors, while the suitcases sprouted into great big pumpkins, which provided John with food through all the peaceful winters that followed.

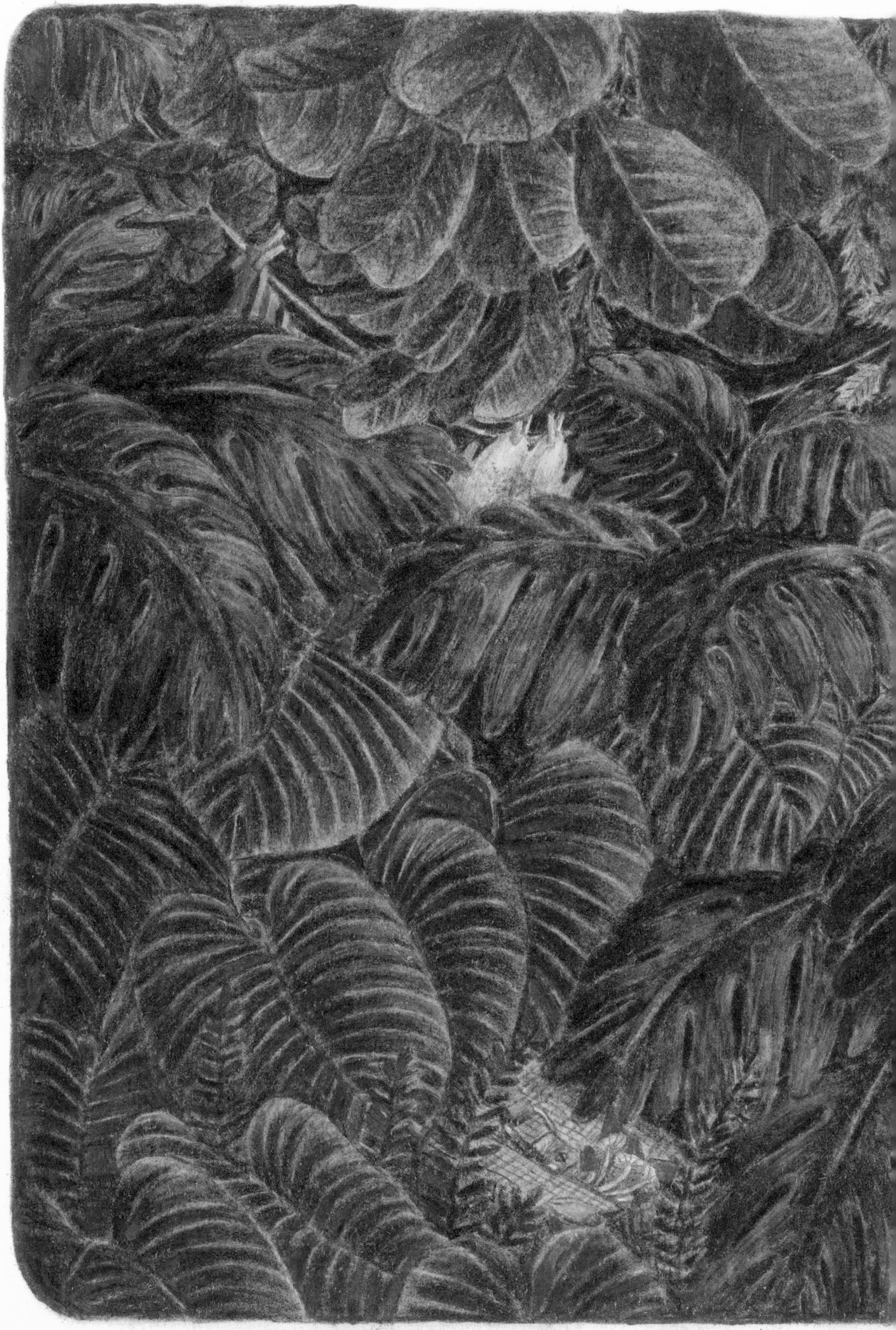

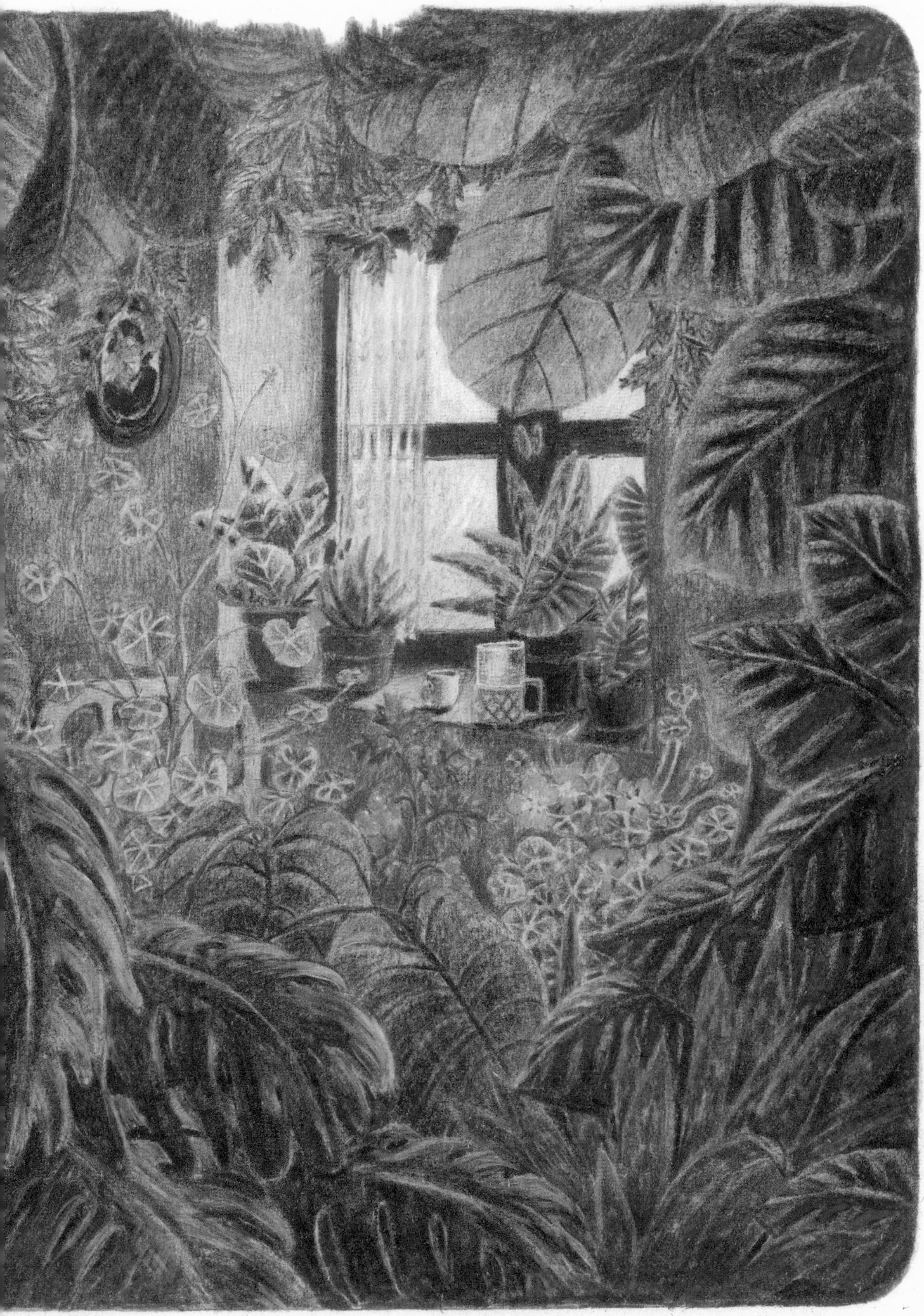

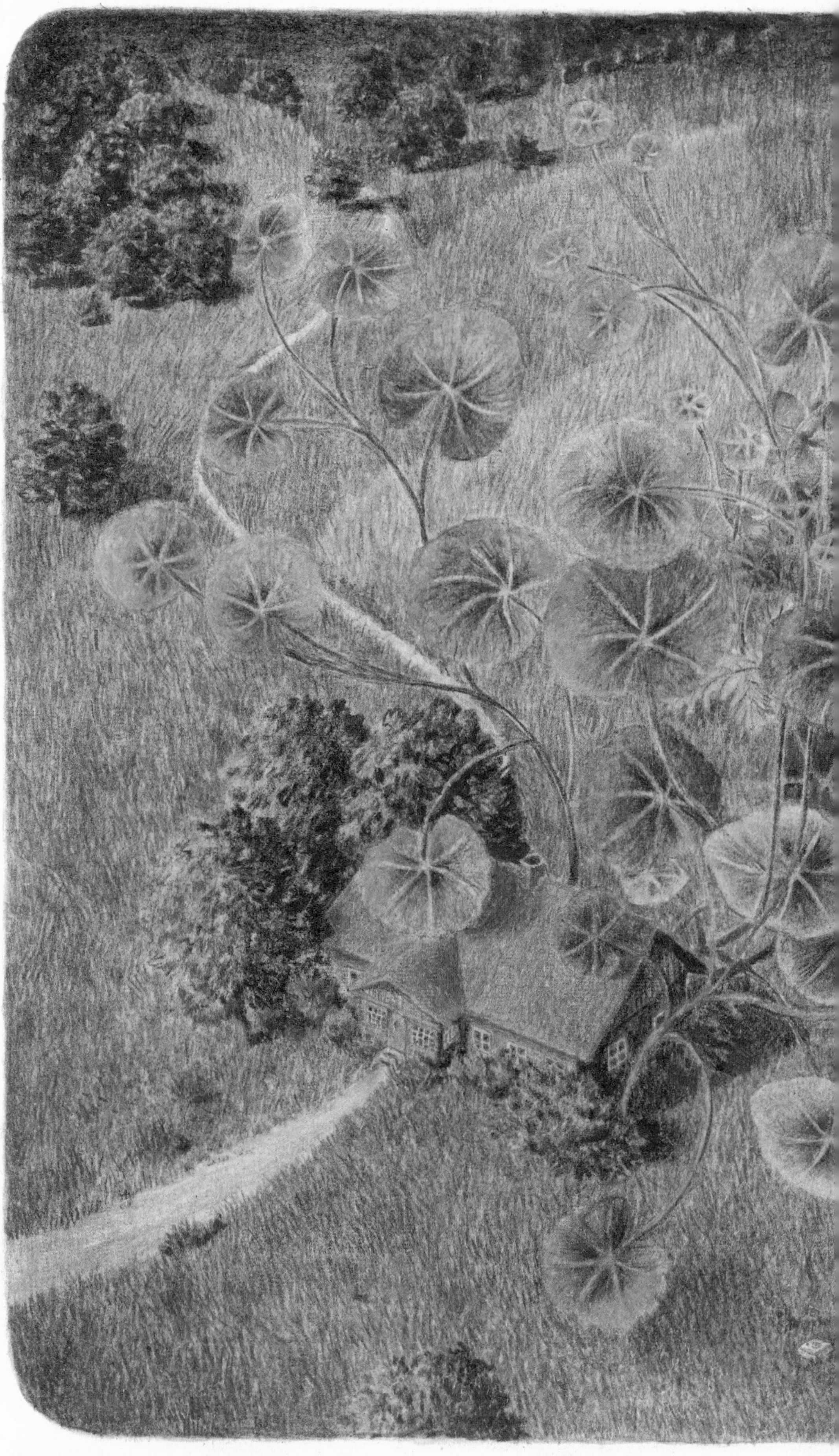

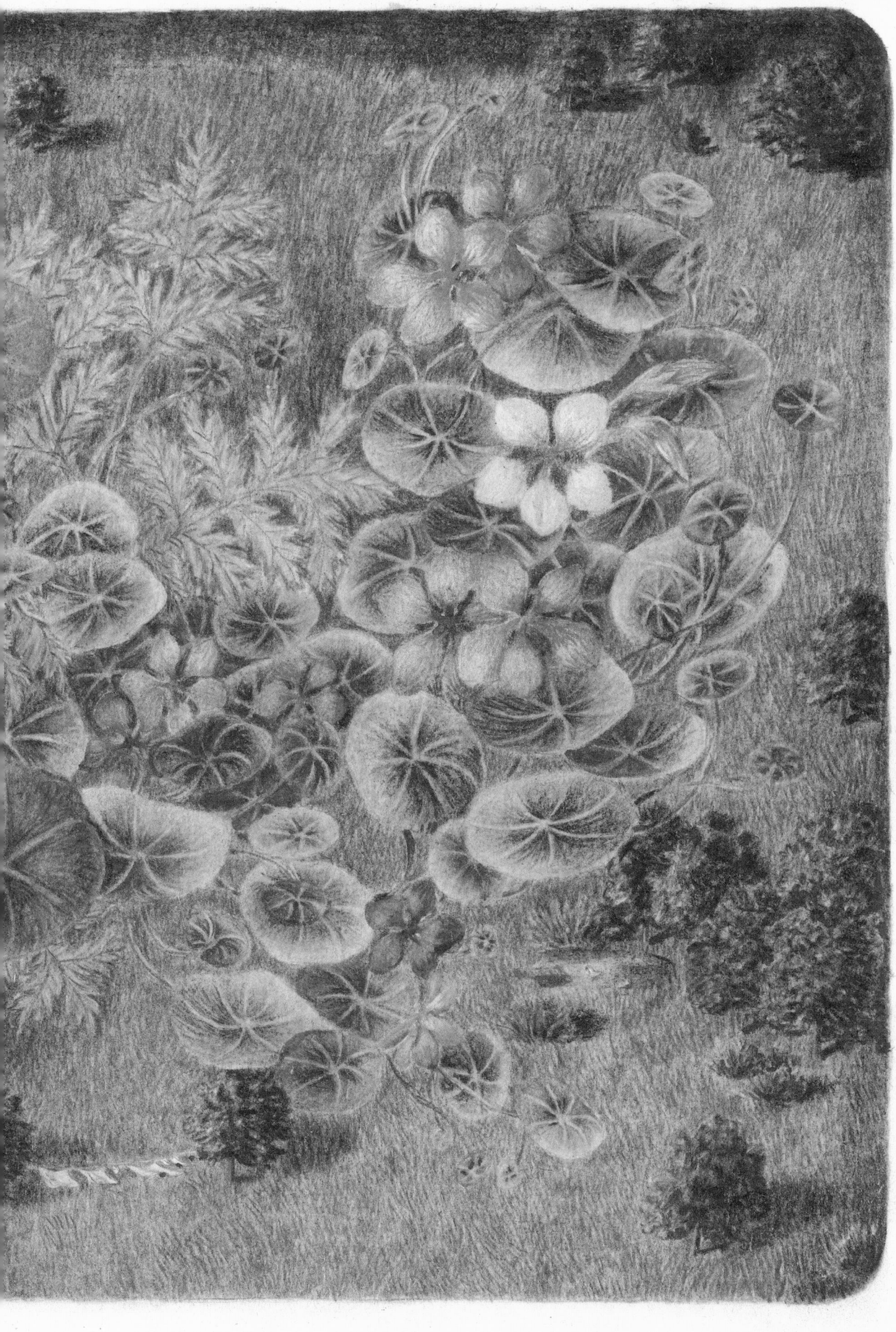

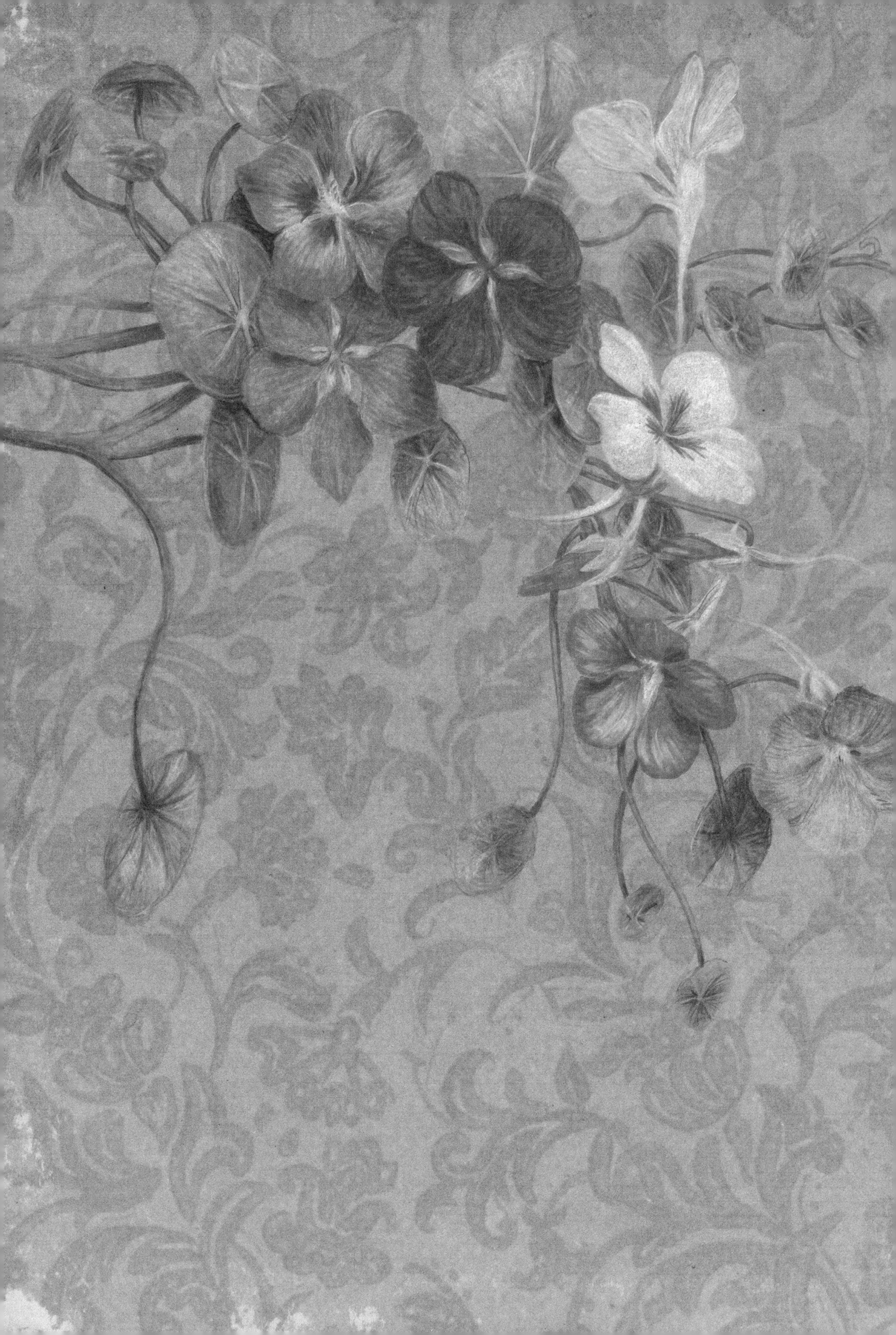